HUMANITY
IS
THE
DEVIL

an anti-novel by
Jordan Krall

HUMANITY IS THE DEVIL

JORDAN KRALL

Morbidbooks Is A Grotesque Bizarro Ballet Where The Most Profane Things Occur. An Impious And Perverse Dwelling Of Dark Revulsion. A Cozy Cottage Where Torture Porn And Brutal Bible Tales Are Devised. A Quiet Place To Relax And Spin Tales Of Depravity And Wickedness. A Halfway House For The Disturbed Where Rules No Longer Apply. A Safe Haven For Deviant Serial Killers To Hatch Their Wretched Schemes. Bring Your Pets.
The Tasty Ones Are Always Welcome.

https://www.morbidbooks.wordpress.com

Acknowledgements

I'd like to thank the following people for their support of this particular project: The Rev, Philip LoPresti, Seb Doubinsky, and Vincenzo Bilof.

-Jordan Krall

HUMANITY IS THE DEVIL

PROLOGUE

Everyone knows about Abraxas.

Yeah, the rooster head. Three hundred and sixty-five. So what? It's almost a joke now. Abraxas this and Abraxas that. Soda cans. Cereal boxes. The beginning. The letter 'A' is the easiest thing to discover. Same thing with Aleph. But there's more. There's always more.

Seth prepares the bomb. He's always the one. He's good at it. He's a master of his craft. A master of many crafts, really. Bomb-making just happens to be his favorite. He relishes the chemicals, the wiring, the computerized chaos of explosives, demolition, destruction, the sparks.

The glorious sparks.

Seth knows about Abraxas. Of course he does.

Doesn't everyone?

"It's finished," he says. The other men look at him, nod in approval, in admiration. He's led them through many tough times. Most of them could be defined as "acts of terror" but Seth wouldn't agree. They were his acts, yes, but he didn't consider them terrible. They were, as he often told his men, simple acts of "infinite, majestic, and limitless light" and "sparks of wisdom manufactured through violence" and then he would laugh. He loves the imagery. He loves the light.

The limitless, limitless light.

PART ONE

"Satan is free for His work is done. Satan is no longer the Devil, for He has passed the poison on to that which chose to take it and become it. Now there is nothing more evil in the universe than man. His world is Hell, and he himself the Devil."

-The Process Church of the Final Judgment

HUMANITY IS THE DEVIL

I. RELIGIOUS EXPERIENCE DISORDER

Seth kneels and prays.

"Oh, even through the din, the pitter-patter of horse hooves and screaming gongs, through the haze of celestial opiate smoke curling and uncurling amidst the lead colored trees whose leaves crack under the pressure of the baragouin's wind, I can hear the pitter-patter, pitter-patter, pitter-patter of the puppets. I hear the clashing cymbals, ringing gongs, post-haste. Listening to the balductum of the gnathonic elders and I vomit onto the chipped paint on the windowsill. Pardon my barrage of skimble-skamble! I turn the television off and watch the metallic media atrocity."

As far as he can tell, Seth's prayer goes unanswered. But this is okay. He is used to it.

"Forever and ever and ever, Amon, Ammo, *Amen*."

II. CALLIPYGIAN IMPLOSION

You take out as many people as possible. If they move, you shoot. That's it. Shoot at anything that moves. Don't hesitate. Don't doubt yourself. Just squeeze the trigger. It's pretty easy once you get the hang of it. Once you get the hang out of knowing that the world is corrupt, people are corrupt, people are just sad little manikins, not exactly puppets, not exactly animals, just ugly shells with just a spark of a spark inside.

In the beginning…

Friday night at the shopping mall.

Eleven ways inside…not counting service doors.

One security office located by the east entrance.

Six officers on duty.

Tasers but no guns.

Lazy in their routines.

Predictable.

Easy to outsmart and overpower.

We are bringing two duffel bags of explosives.

We are bringing two boxes of literature to leave behind at the areas where there is minimal impact.

We are bringing fourteen automatic rifles, sixteen handguns, and a dozen grenades.

The grenades were an inspired choice. Seth thought they would remind people of rocks being thrown as they have done centuries ago, before gunpowder, and the public may be transported, even if only for a split second, to biblical times.

I asked Seth if we should maybe bring swords as well being they would also be quite symbolic but he said that they were too unwieldy for the assault and would counteract our effectiveness during the event. Maybe but I still think having swords would strike some sort of fear into the Demiurge's manikins.

Fear is a powerful weapon.

That's what I've always thought.

Now...

You put the DVD into the player and watch Seth give a lecture: *You are but a clay vessel. You exist only to hold what is given to you, what is put into you by the Designer of Corruption, the Grand Builder, the Demiurge. I will empty you of your broken light. I will leave you in the desert cave until the purest sparks, purest light flows from your eyes, from your heart and then and only then will I break the seal on the box that imprisons Sophia.*

The DVD freezes so you can't watch the rest.

Watch some videos on the internet. Video footage. Suburban home. Lights off. Smoke rising from basement window.

Inside.

Twelve year old boy, battered, raped, mutilated.

Five year old sister, battered, raped, mutilated.

Forty-five year old mother, battered raped, mutilated.

Forty-six year old father, battered, mutilated, shot.

There's broken glass. Television on. Cartoons. Sledgehammer. Tooth fairy. Milk. Dirty laundry. Bookshelf. Dog licking blood. Holy Holy Holy. Preposterous alibi. Dawn gaping. Knife wound viscera deep dark red.

Outside.

Proceed as planned.

III. SORRY PIGLET

In your morbidity you have painted your bedroom black. This is not surprising. You want to lie on your bed and dream of Tillich's Paradox. You breathe deeply from green bottles.

I'll survive your attempts to murder me!

So far we have about three possible dates, three windows of opportunity. We have enough, well, just enough time to gather our resources, write our documents, upload them, watch the reactions, record the reactions, and pray. Never stop praying, man, never stop. Pray without ceasing, that's what you have to remember.

Pray without ceasing.

The black paint is peeling and underneath I can see the rainbow you splattered up there when you were a child, when you weren't so morbid. It's okay, quite okay, because sooner or later we all tear down the veils and see the real filth hanging from the rafters. There are *spirits* in the rafters!

Spirits!

In the rafters!

When your mother found the magazines under the bed, what did she say? Did she say you were disgusting? Did she say you disgusted her? Or was she speechless? Was she? Come on, you can tell me.

Did she say anything to you or did she just look at you with that disapproving disgust? You sicken me. You sicken yourself. What kind of person would look at this? How did I even give birth to you? Kill yourself. You know where my pills are. Kill yourself. You have a belt. Do it. Do it so you can't disgust me anymore. Hang yourself. Cut yourself. You're disgusting and you disgust me.

Your dream of the paradox is still here. You won't succeed in murdering me.

IV. BORDER CROSSING

Unplanned execution, swollen mouth, police report, kidnapping, fuselage, mentality.

The black-gloved blade moves slowly across the neck…spurt, spurt, sexual overload, newspaper articles, internet countdown, release sparks, reserve your judgment, eyes lock up, outside of Walmart, sell your baby for rent money. Trashcan lullaby. Dumpster blowjob. Minimal amount of spillage. Stained t-shirt. Mustard semen. Black eye. Welfare check.

Multiple shots fired, multiple authors killed, disemboweled journalists hanging from the bridge.
(YOU REPORT THINGS AND YOU GET WHAT THEY GET)
Schoolgirls slaughtered in a haze of gunfire, axe hacks, poisoning, sexual snapshots, upskirts, put on display in hospitals, locks, bolts, tattoos of phone numbers, underage victims, splattered Gnostic cumshot. Pistols. Pistis. Elongated eye socket. Smothering infant killer. Hail problem solver, childcare nightmare. Trauma to the body. Trauma, not an accident, size of a fist, an adult fist, bury the screamer under the trailer.

"Everyday is like Sunday…"

V. RITUALS

Seth places the clay tablets on the stove, turns the knob, and watches the fury of the earth split open, split the walls, ceiling. A mighty sight to behold – The Christian Army of Southern Rape, the mutilated remains of young women, a mighty Christus.

There is a reason for everything. No doubt about that. I'm not saying GOD has any reasoning, no sir, but I'm saying there is some universal reasoning somewhere, some latent logic that is so far beyond our understand of how things work. That little girl found in the suitcase. She was violated with some sharp object during her final minutes alive. There's reason in that. Somewhere. I just know it. Does GOD know it? Maybe.

Seth retreats into his cuneiform clown costume. He logs into his website, turns the camera on, turns his retreat into revenue. Clown sparks, clown spurts, clown Christus, Christus clown, Christ the Killer, online transactions, dead sea server.

Connection complete.

VI. CIRCULAR TEMPLES

A subtle surprise as he opens the book: These are my plans. There are my strategies and techniques for tearing down the Demiurge's gate. Fortress made of fragile clay, open dirty ugly clay pits in Kennedy Park, open wound dirty ugly underage remote control sycophant, phantom molester. You can't see the blast, what a relief, pull it down, man as goblin performs in pornographic corners of factories, schools, and the man writes down his grocery list in Coptic.

No refunds.

No returns.

No possible escape.

He duct-taped her wrists, ankles, tore off her clothes, stabbed her dozens of times, inserted his beer-stained cock into the wounds, this is his smiling, this is his childhood sweetheart, plastic forms outside the cave, vanity, vanity, all is vanity.

I can preach all day, all night. No skin off my back. Tell it to the whores, you scumbag. The cunts can't stop calling me. I smash my phone. I don't want to hear their voices. They aren't alive anymore. Who gives a shit? Not me. Surely, not me. Ugly clay-faced clowns, those filthy sluts and gaping fags. No refunds, man. No returns. This isn't a fucking department store. You reap what you sow. You weak, weak sorry excuse for a human being. Selling kids. You sell kids. You trade kids. You use the Internet to sell kids. How much money do you make?

No returns. No possible escape. No talking. No screaming. No Coptic graffiti on the walls of your cell. Your childhood memories: cocaine and pornography and a camcorder. Ashtray mouth.

Dirty gate reveals ugly yard.

Mow the lawn.

VII. LAST MAJOR CONSEQUENCE

Automatic rifle pornographic magazines, the construction worker thought about kids, created his own model train set, constructed houses for plastic boys, smashed them, video recorded the molestation, stashed them in his mother's garage, volunteered to coach Little League.

Seth sneaks into the man's house.

Slaughters them all.

Sets the explosive.

The house, not unexpectedly, explodes.

Somewhere a television is on:

"You're such a cut-up!"

"You ain't seen nothin' yet!"

"You're such a clown."

"Nah, nah, I'm not a funny guy. Not at all."

"Soon you will be… haha!"

"Haha!"

VIII. THOMAS

Maybe we should reconsider our plan. After all, if all evil flows from above from the Demiurge's beyond, what good will it do to (IF YOU ARE DOUBTING OUR PURPOSE THEN YOU ARE AS CORRUPT AS THE STRUCTURES WE CONDEMN)

I'm not really doubting. It's just that I'm so used to over-thinking my decisions in life. I'm so stressed out all the time. I can't even hold a job because I can't take the stress. I can't take the decision making. I can't make any decision ever. I've pretty much resigned myself to letting other people make the decisions for me. It's much easier that way. I guess it does sort of leave me blameless. Whatever happens is not because of me but because of the decision that someone else made for me.

I don't have much integrity or inner fortitude or whatever you call it. I don't like conflict. I just want to be left alone and neutral. But this plan, this plan that Seth came up with really spoke to me, spoke to my soul (maybe?) and I can't help but follow through but still... I'm sort of having second thoughts but I wouldn't really call them doubts. I just think a lot. I just sit in my room and think. It's a full time job, really.

IX. PRELUDE TO A PRIVATE PARTY

Falcone put the DVD into the computer and started the movie. I sat there, not impressed so far. I heard Falcone was hardcore but so far nothing he had shown me was new. All your typical underground footage: war atrocity footage (Vietnam, Gulf War, Bosnia, Afghanistan, Iraq), footage of idiotic gang members recording their sloppy drive-by shootings on their camera phones. Other clips were Mexican mafia epics, Eastern European gyno-torture, South American pedo-snuff. All extremely disgusting but nothing actually new. Nothing that wasn't out there on hundreds of thousands of computers. All of it a glimpse into what humans do when they run out of their inmost light.

Falcone's last DVD started...and I broke down in tears. My heart dropped down, smashed and alone in the universe, no stars, no galaxies, nothing, nothing, nothing, nothing, nothing.

My bowels loosened and I gave up on everything: humanity, God, myself.

I looked over at Falcone.

He was masturbating.

X. TELEVISED

"Do you have any suspects in custody?"

"At this time we have no suspects in custody but we do have a few we are looking at as persons of interest."

"Why did it take so long for authorities to respond to the 911 calls?"

"I have no comment on that except to say that we followed procedure."

"There have been reports of at least five men in white military gear near the scene. Are those accurate reports?"

"I can't comment on that at this time."

"Is there any connection to last month's mall shootings?"

"Right now, we can't say."

"Is there any connection to January's bombing?"

"Right now no comment."

"What about the reports that a duffel bag was found at the scene?"

"Yes, a bag was recovered."

"Is it true that the bag contained illegal pornography in addition to ammunition?"

"I can't comment on that."

"There were reports that child pornography was found."

"Again, I can't comment on that."

"To go back to the person of interest, is that related to the reports of a gunman last night at Ruysbroeck Center?"

"That was an unrelated incident that's currently under investigation."

XI. PISTIS BLOW-UP

Conversation between friends.

"I duct taped the bitch's mouth shut."

"Doin' it in style, are you?"

"Couldn't find a ball gag."

"That happens."

"Hog-tied her, too. She squirmed. I took pictures."

"Video, too?"

"Yeah, of course."

"Nice."

SAM SCRAWLS HIS NAME ON THE BATHROOM STALL DOOR. 'GOING TO BLOW UP THE PLACE / WIN THE DUEL'

I didn't know what he said. I didn't know that it was going to be exactly like that but regardless, it's not like I had any other choice. These things happen, these things happen to the best of us and even the worst which is perhaps my case, I don't know, you can be the judge of that.

I walked home, stopped at the Knights of Columbus and stood outside in front of the statue of Mary there surrounded by neon, encased in concrete or whatever. I've never been much into praying but I figured it wouldn't hurt. Sooner or later, even the Demiurge's world seems comforting. DON'T LET ANYONE KNOW I SAID THAT.

I've scrawled my messages on bathroom walls all across New Jersey. I'm hoping someone is keeping a record of them. I imagine there has to be at least one person who is intrigued enough.

I can hope.

I can pray.

I can pray without ceasing.

XII. REVELATIONS

When I was eight years old, I fell off my bicycle and hit my head. I don't think I was actually knocked unconscious but I do remember seeing things in front of me. Stars twinkling and then these things...the best way I can describe them is to say that it looked like black giraffes riding bicycles up and down the street. A few minutes later my father found me, picked me up, and took me back to the house where my mother tended to my wounds. I've never seen those black giraffes again.

XIII. CONFESSION OF A SPIDER

"No doubt about it, we are dealing with terrorists here. On first look, their ideology seems unusual in relation to terrorism but it has all the same characteristics. The unfortunate thing is that they are gaining more sympathy by the day thanks to the Internet and their video and blog posts. It's pretty ridiculous how ignorant the public can be, how misinformed, so willing to believe a small destructive minority instead of their elected officials. Quite frankly I'm tired of this shit, of having to convince the public that *we're* the good guys. I got into law enforcement because I wanted to do make a difference, as corny as that sounds. I wasn't really expecting the political side of it, the press conferences, the ass kissing, the excuse making, and all the shit I have to go through just to do my job. Sometimes I just feel like giving up, you know, and sometimes I even empathize with the other side. I mean, I guess if I was fed up enough, and was at my wit's end, I might end up doing something like these guys, you know, set a bomb somewhere, go crazy, shoot some people to release my rage and frustration. I guess everyone is capable of something like that. Just takes some self-control to hold that shit back. But I can understand it. A man can only take so much shit before he blows. Even a normal guy. But if you take a guy who hasn't had a normal life, then well, what the hell has he got to lose? I don't know. I'm pretty close to retirement and I'm hoping I can just close this case and go out quietly, you know. I don't know, I just don't now."

XIV. THINGS WE WANT

Seth leans back on the couch, puts his hand on Gerald's knee.

He says, "Listen, I know it's difficult for you to get involved with this stuff so fast. I'm not unsympathetic. I understand how extreme the transition is. I've been in that place. I also respect your decision to join us. It's not just an intellectual decision you had to make. It was a spiritual one, a psychological one. I know it took you a long time to come to the decision to not only believe what we do but to join us in our actions or as I like to call them, our 'acts'. I like that word. It brings to mind something biblical but also theatrical. That's pretty appropriate considering the true corrupt architecture of the world, of this existence, the reality we interact in. It's all theater set up by the Demiurge and so…our 'acts' help to bring things down to a pure level. So when you're in doubt, when you are like some little Thomas, just remember that we all have sparks and doubt only serves to extinguish them. We don't want that, do we? No, we don't want that at all."

XV. MESSAGE MOLESTATION

There is a predator erasing the blueprints of corruption. Laudate Deum!

Forms, nonforms, void.

He's hiding around the playground. Can you see him? He has a camera. He has a notebook. He has a pen.

The "I" that observes is not the "I" that experiences. Rip your emotions off like your clothes and bask naked in the potential sparks of G_D.

You're obsessed.

The predator is still there. You can think about him all you want but he still will not acknowledge your existence. You are a ghost to him. You are all ghosts to him now.

Good luck catching him.

Forms, nonforms, void.

Letters in the mail detailing the abuse.

Polaroid pictures. (Does anyone actually use a Polaroid camera anymore? Maybe. Maybe it's something nostalgic for them, a tradition that they are slow to move away from. Maybe it reminds them of a simpler time, a time when they didn't have to worry about their pictures being traced electronically.)

XVI. PINPOINT

Seth confides in his therapist.

"I'm not going to say it all boils down to my mom and dad…but sometimes I think that's what it's about, my feelings of helplessness and resentment towards people in authority."

"Well, we tend to put our parents in a particular position wherein we expect too much from them. Remember, parents are people who just happened to have had children. They aren't special human beings."

"I know that. I think I just have expected more from them or maybe… something different. I don't know."

"What in particular has been on your mind?"

"My mom was overprotective when I was a kid so I didn't really get to experience much, not what boys usually do. I didn't get to feel that adrenaline rush so I think I've been trying to make up for it now."

"Did something in particular make you think of this?"

"I think it was when I was watching some kids skateboard down the street. I mean, it looked dangerous but I couldn't help but feel jealous of these thirteen, fourteen year old kids."

"So you've felt like you had to do some sort of risky behavior?"

"I don't know if I'd call it risky...that makes me think of promiscuous sex and doing drugs."

"How would you describe your actions?"

"Maybe...daring...important..."

"Important how?"

"Just in the scheme of things. It's hard to explain."

"You know, that's why some people join the military, to get that rush as well as do something important. Have you thought about that? Joining the military?"

"No...I'd never do that."

"Why not?"

"For ideological reasons."

"So what do you do in your life that you label as important or daring?"

"I do... I guess you'd call it.....charity work... with my church."

"Well, that's good. Religion is often a good way to satisfy certain needs we have. What is it you do that's daring?"

"Some of our charity work takes us into some dangerous areas."

"Oh? And is that the reason why you do it? The main reason?"

"Because it's dangerous?"

"Yeah."

"No, I don't think so. I mean…we, all of us, have purpose when it comes to what we do. It's not risk-taking for the sake of risk-taking."

"That's good to hear. Risky behavior often makes us feel even more helpless in the long run. When we start to lose too much of our inhibitions we can often start losing control of everything else."

"I think I'm in control."

"How do your parents figure into this?"

"I feel like…there are residual feelings there, an underlying resentment because of them. I can't shake it. I don't consciously blame them for anything yet I can't whole-heartedly… love them or get close to them. I don't know if that makes sense."

"It makes perfect sense."

"And it prevents me from speaking to them. I mean, if they call I'll usually answer but I don't call them or visit unless they insist and even then I dread it."

"Why? Does something specific happen when you visit?"

"Nothing in particular. It's just awkward. I close up…emotionally, I mean. I can't relax. I don't talk to them about anything real, anything significant."

"And how do *they* act?"

"Normal, I guess. I mean…for them. My mom dotes on me and my dad is a bit standoffish but will try to make conversation. Most of the time when I visit, he asks me for a favor."

"Like what?"

"Just if I could help him with yard work or pick up something at the store for him."

"How do you respond to this?"

"I try to make an excuse. If I can't, I agree but I just feel like I barely have a choice."

"Does he know you feel this way?"

"No, I think he's pretty oblivious."

"Have you tried talking to him about how you feel?"

"No."

"Why not?"

"I just don't think it would do any good. It'd be more trouble than it's worth."

"How so?"

"It would be awkward and it would start a fight."

"Why? What would he say?"

"I think he'd just accuse me of being selfish, not being a good son."

"Is that what you're afraid of? Being viewed as not being a good son?"

"I don't think so. I mean, I already know I'm not a good son. I just don't want to fight about it."

XVII. INSIDE THE MARTYRDOME

The Circs, as we'll call them, a group of them swarmed a political rally, hitting people with clubs, and responded to the police's orders to stop by getting even more violent. Shots were fired and about ten Circs were dead just as they planned, just as they wished.

What I remember from that day is the happiness they seemed to show as they were being attacked. It's like these Circs were asking for death. It was weird.

I admire them in a way. I've love to be able to greet death with that much passion. It's inspiring. I've watched plenty of death videos on the Internet and I've probably seen hundreds of people being killed and only a few were that inspiring, you know. There are some people who embrace dying so wonderfully… It's almost akin to those who embrace killing with such passion. You have to respect that. You have to respect a person who lives life with that sort of passion. The fact that they can kill someone and find joy in it… or die with a smile on their face. It's really pretty inspirational. It's more inspirational than any sermon or feel-good story you hear on the news.

XVIII. MEXICAN STUNT MAN

So about twenty-five of them went to the bridge and hung themselves. It was quite a sight, really, seeing all these men (and two women) hanging from the bridge like retired marionettes.

Why'd they do it?

Why does anyone do it?

Why does anyone do anything?

You're too young to understand.

YOU ARE PRACTICALLY A CHILD.

Twenty-five martyrs swing, swing, swing low, close to the water, close to the briny water, choke on it.

CHOKE ON IT GAG XXX LIVE SHOW

All he did as a child was draw vampire comics, black and white, eating spiders, hideous creatures, poppycock, stupid words splashing in and out.

In the backroom of the porno place, a few girls were kept as (basically) receptacles for anything the men wanted to dispose of. The men would pay the guy up front $50 and get fifteen minutes with one of the trash girls.

Hydra NYC, a final solution, a death squad, beginnings of a cult of Christ, Christ who is not a stranger, Christ who is not a man but who is a man, touches your faces, your hearts, molests daycare sycophants, elaborate court order, extensive investigation tunnels beneath the building, smuggling victims pale, tied up, swollen, gapes, ugly reminders of relaxed laws, restricting dogma, stations of the cross, FM/AM, slow motion endless slaughter bridge cult, birth death conspiracy, maybe SM/BD. Mexican cunt squad. Black punch. Christ is a gorgon.

XIX. REPEATED REPORTS

Seth figures if he can't just wear them down enough for them to SEE (opened eyes, light, body light) and perhaps adopt the PURPOSE...

He eats melons and absorbs the light within.

Murder is... what?

Rape is... what?

Abuse is... what?

Definitions are nothing but manmade nonsense to defend the weak. There is no illness but the refusal to bend to the shape of the light. For what is the shape of the light?

You are but a clay vessel. You exist only to hold what is given to you, what is put into you by the Designer of Corruption, the Grand Builder, the Demiurge. I will empty you of your broken light. I will leave you in the desert cave until the purest sparks, purest light flows from your eyes, from your heart and then and only then will I break the seal on the box that imprisons Sophia.

We do what we want. Everyone everywhere does what they want. We do what we want. Everything is dangerous. Everything at all times. Everything is dangerous at all times. Murder is nothing so adopt my purpose.

XX. INDOCTRINATION TRIMARITAS

There is a lot to be said about the murders and their relationship to the exegetical posts that have been published on the internet from May 2000 to June 20XX.

Though we cannot exactly place a direct chain of causation into place, hindsight has allowed us to reinvigorate our study into this movement and gather evidence that supports the theory that the posts themselves were, in some yet to be explained, were the spark that lit the fire that resulted in the murders (and the various other acts of violence).

In all, there were 3,148 internet posts ranging from three-hundred words each to forty-two thousand. This collection, this exegesis of baroque extrapolation found only in the most nonsensical of texts was not only posted in English but in Spanish, German, Latin, and Coptic. A few were posted only in Hebrew (these posts, now known as the *Aliphaen Texts*, were only published between August 2005 and October 2005).

Though the website domain has expired, the entirety of its contents has been archived by Rutgers University under the care of Dr. Sven Teleborian.

Dr. Teleborian speculates that the text (when it was in electronic form) had been altered by the original researchers for reasons unknown. If that is the case, it will be a difficult task determining which of the text is original to the author/s.

XXI. ONE PLUS ZERO

"That's when I pulled my weapon, told the suspect to drop his, and to get face down on the ground with his hands out."

"Then what happened?"

"He proceeded to approach me, slowly at first at which time I again ordered him down. He then rushed forward. I fired two shots and hit the suspect in the left shoulder and arm. He kept coming so I made the decision to fire one more shot which entered his abdomen. The suspect then collapsed."

"Did you feel like your life was in danger at any point?"

"Of course."

"The suspect was only armed with a wooden club, is that correct?"

"Yes."

"Does your department issue you taser guns in addition to a firearm?"

"I didn't have my taser at the time."

"But your department *does* issue them?"

"Yes."

"And do you think if you had your taser and had used it instead of your firearm the suspect would still be alive?"

"I can't speculate on that."

"Did the suspect say anything while he was approaching?"

"Not when he was approaching at first but when he rushed me he said something. I don't exactly remember what. It sounded like another language. Latin maybe. I don't know."

"No further questions."

XXII. SOZIALPOLITIK/SOZIALMORD

"The physician is the greatest mass murderer of the poor in the history of mankind…Thus begins the vigilante justice, the terror of the medical society in the pluralistic chaos of criminality. But terror can only be extirpated with counter-terror, and whoever denies me the protection of the law forces the cudgel into my hand." – Walter Seifert

Un Chau Street Estate, 1982. The man was ugly. I remember that much. I was hurting, my arm and chest and the man was ugly. In the backroom there was a pile of soiled magazines from Denmark. Lolita shit. Approved by the Church of England. Costumes. Classifieds. PO Boxes. Attitudes toward sexuality. Ugly men sharing an apartment. Local kids. Swimming pool. Shallow end. Diagnosis. Pills. Coke. Cum. Plastic wrap. Shit films. Gay rape of married men. Fisting.

Sometimes he starts fires. Sometimes he relinquishes control to the archons.

"I am reasonable certain that this young man has a serious psychosexual problem, that he is using the technique of denial…"

Child psychologist dissecting brains. Indecent assault. What was your role in this?

DID YOU EVER TOUCH THAT KID?

XXIII. I AM WAITING FOR THE CHARIOT

Seth pushes the lawn mower, grimacing and resenting his agreement to help. His father is in the doorway, watching. "Make sure you get near the edges, too."

"Okay." Seth curses under his breath.

The edges, edges, the edges of the yard. The long grass always forgotten, always left long because it was a pain in the ass to maneuver the mower in such a way as to get every piece of grass.

Seth wishes he was somewhere else. He rolls his eyes into the back of his head and imagines.

He is waiting for the chariot.

The chariot arrives: fourteen wheels within thirty-six circles, spirals, distorted squares among bloated stars expanding, contracting, dying, cloud bursts, ink blots, the chariot rises from the mountain, smoke form and void, glass horizon breaks into stone, soothes the firmament. Rain breaks, lightning forms a cloud, a mind, the fortress expands, restricts the expanse, bloated cascading faces blocking the view, laudate sol, liquid blocks within the chariot's edge…the edge…edge…

"Get the edges, son."

OKAY.

XXIV. REPORT ON PROBABILITY C

Voices we hear.

"There's a guy slaughtering people."

Police: Mom beat infant to death.

It's all in the report.

Burned, decapitated body found.

Boy, 4, found mutilated in clay pit.

You'd think they'd have caught someone by now.

Sooner or later everyone and everything defies logic and contributes to the banana porcupine sunspot veil pottery bombs.

Later that day, the suspect assaulted the victim.

Violated live on the internet.

Her own daughter.

Garbage bags.

Suitcase.

Lubricant.

VHS tapes labeled "Michelle 6" "Jessica 5"

"We need to have some sympathy for him. He's sick. He needed help. We failed him. Society failed him. What he did to those kids…it was a result of his own abuse."

At the hands of the archons, no doubt.

"There's a kid slaughtering kids."

XXV. EXOTIC MEAT

Kuchisake-onna, my pretty. You were there when I bombed the police headquarters. You were there when I shot up the schoolyard. You were there when I drowned those kids.

But now... Now where are you? I fear so much without you. I fear.

Hey Hey Hanako-san Our song is on the jukebox and we're dancing to it like we always do on Friday nights 11:14 AM.

I recall you took photographs of the schoolyard stabbings. You developed the photos yourself. You always had so much talent. What did you do with the pictures? You sent them to a magazine. What magazine? You sent them to one that caters to your type of obsession.

Look at the kids! Look at the big old stab wounds in their tiny little bodies! What sort of society can give birth to this?

It is unfortunate that the authorities were alerted to the mail you sent. I curse them, all of them. You should not be locked up in a hell hole with common scum. I send you my love, my love. Where are you? I fear so much without you, without you I fear you.

XXVI. NAME NAMES

When I became cognizant of the overwhelming ignorance of my family, there wasn't much for me to do but reestablish a foundation on which I can build my own genetic legacy. Most of what I've learned from life I've learned from books though I wouldn't consider myself a scholar or anything close to it. In fact, I don't understand most of what I read which is obviously a symptom of my unfortunate inheritance of substandard intellect. I'm fully aware that many people have it so much worse though this doesn't stop me from lamenting my position. Why should it? There will always be someone who has it worse and there will always be someone who has it better, so much better. So that should not stop me from discontent and the quest (the mission!) for a new biological and intellectual destiny. No, I cannot stop.

XXVII. PRISTINE GRACE

Seth walks up to the automatic doors.
They open.
He walks through the doorway.
He sees the cashiers
Their faces bored, plain, somewhat ugly.
Seth opens fire.
They drop.
Cigarettes and batteries explode.
Voices.
Shouts.
Is this for real?
Shit yeah, this is for real.
Emergency exit doors open.
Fire alarm.
Mommy!
Voices.
Run!
Seth sprays again.
Random.
Here, here, pray.
Get down.
Voices.
What?
What is that?
Who?

Is this for real?
Shit yeah, this is for real.
Get down.
Watch out.
Please god!
God!
Where's my son?
Run!
There's a shooter!
Did someone call 911?
I did!
Get down!
God!
Oh my God!
My Father who art in…
Is this for real?
Shit yeah..
Voices.
Get down.
Pray.
Pray!
Pray without ceasing!

XXVIII. BAPTIST

Manifesto.

Trinity. Pastor Martin raped his daughter.
Split her open.
Hymns.
Cocaine.
Pornography.
Repentance.
Suffering.
Prayer meeting. Sit here. Talk. Spare the rod. Sermon on the mount. Blast. Bathroom. Deacon. Plastic bags. Very bad day. Hermit. Twelve tables. Feast. Blow up.

Pastor Martin's brother (also a pastor) raped his niece.
Hymns.
Meth.
Blackout.
Tithes.
Come down. Dog hair. White heart. False face. Trinity Baptist. Anal scars. Favorite song. Dome light. Happy. Raspberry strudel.

Predestination.

XXIX. BAIT

She was tied up like a fish. Kept like that. Ate like that. Raped like that. Twelve years. Long years. Rope burns. Inverted cross of the hidden Christians of Edo. Machine shop massacre. Endgame flashpoint fireworks. Let bygones be bygones. Why won't you write me back?

She was tied up like a carp.

How do you tie up carp?

How do you breathe with a plastic bag over your head?

I'm not a scholar or anything. Where are you? I fear so much without you. Look at the kids! I don't know anything. Obviously a symptom of my unfortunate inheritance. No, I cannot stop. I cannot be responsible for my ACTIONS and though I'm fairly certain the FINAL stage of my solution to this.

Deadbolt. Crawlspace. Parenthood. Pipe bomb. Children's services. Blindfold. Court date. Lubrication. Watch the footage for blurred-out faces. So young, so unknown. Have you been a victim, too?

He opens fire. They drop. Voices. Random. Tied up like a fish. Camcorder. Hog. Basement. Birthday. Fuck toy. Christian. Regret.

HUMANITY IS THE DEVIL

She was tied up like a fucking carp.

XXX. EMOTIVE

Conduct disorder. Oppositional defiant disorder. Disruptive behavior disorder. Adjustment disorder. A transient father. Low birth weight. Unusual reactions to pain. Low frustration tolerance. Animal abuse. Lack of remorse. Lack of empathy. Classical conditioning. Operant. Cruel and unusual cruising. Role models. Same factors. Violent films. Ritalin. Clallam Bay. Short attention span. Appropriate social behaviors. Murder at Upminster Bridge. Black doodler. Internet chat. Strangers. Clips. How do you tie up carp? Watch out. Where's my kid? Heroin + fentanyl. Weeding out the weak. There is an autistic apocalypse. Classifying each murder until there is release. A giant chart. Shopping mall bloodshed. Behavior problems. Rehabilitation. Low I.Q. and so on…

XXXI. ATRAX

The archons of disorder bless the rest of the upstarts.

Live sex show.

Suburbia.

Jump rope.

Tied up like a carp.

I don't understand. You obviously don't care. You don't give a shit. I don't care what you say or do anymore. You're a coward, a fucking coward and the only way you will get my respect back is if you agree to do what you said you were going to do.

Be a man, shithead. Be a man. Do what you said you were going to do. Follow through with your promises. This is it. This is the real deal. This is the way we solidify our manhood, our humanity, we go berserk.

BE A FUCKING MAN.

We go all in, guns blazing, bombs exploding, throats cut, all spilled blood out of the brains and necks knives homosexual star menstrual stuffed alligator flushed card game. Gotta have flies or motion sickness. Gotta have a blanket to cover the wounds. Hey Seth do it. I'm ready. The locks are broken. The locks are throats.

I'M SLITTING THEM NOW.

XXXII. SUNSHINE

Raymond David Garcia, 33, of the Bronx, stabbed a woman. How many times? The coroner says anywhere from 45 to 50 times. Mostly to the groin. Some to the abdomen. It was difficult to determine if there was any sexual assault since the woman's genitals were "devastated" but the stab wounds. No semen was found, however. When questioned by the police, Garcia said, "She was a hot piece of pussy and I had to have her." He is being held without bail.

All of his life, Garcia knew what he wanted to do. He thought about it constantly. When he fucked prostitutes, he imagined that his cock was a knife. He imagined that the prostitute's vagina was an open wound on the body of his mother. That's what he thought about constantly. Almost daily.

He knew he was born to be a destroyer. And that was okay. Everyone had their place in the world.

XXXIII. ALEPH SAYS

I don't like holidays. I don't even like my own birthday. I don't want gifts. I don't want people to say, "Happy Birthday" to me. I hate that. When people say it to me, I want to punch them. I want to hurt them or anyone. I try to stay in my room during any holiday. I hate people acknowledging holidays or any special days. I don't want any attention. I hate getting haircuts because people say, "You got a haircut?" or "Nice haircut" and I hate that. When they say that, I want to cut them. I want to hurt them or anyone. I don't want anyone to say anything to me ever. They say, "Good morning" and I just barely open my mouth. I let out just like a groan or something. I don't want to say anything back to them. They ask me how I am and I don't want to tell them or talk to them at all. When they ask me how I am, I just want to cut them, punch them or hurt them or anyone. I haven't talked to my mother in months even though we live in the same house. I just email her if I need something and she'd learned to email me only if necessary and if it's a pointless message from her I just don't write back. She used to email to remind me to take my medication but she's learned to stop because I would only respond with an email that said, "FUCK

YOU I'M NOT TAKING IT" and so she's learned and hasn't mentioned it. She doesn't mention going to therapy anymore either which is good because that really pisses me off because I hate going and talking to some stupid asshole who doesn't know me or anything about me and who wants to change my personality. There is probably something wrong with my personality but that's just the way I am. There's something wrong but I think everyone has something wrong. No one is perfect. So why should I change? Why can't others change? Just leave me alone and let me stay in my room. Sometimes I go into chatrooms and start arguments and call people "CUNTS" and "FAGGOTS" and just get people to get angry and argue but I always laugh because they don't know who I am and they can't say anything to me that will hurt my feelings. Sometimes I post disgusting pictures in chatrooms, mostly kids chatrooms and stuff, and post pictures of real dead bodies or some sort of gross porn pic with women tied up or something and then I watch people freak out and I laugh and call them "CUNTS" and "FAGGOTS" and then I go back into the chatroom later with a different screen name. Sometimes I get random email addresses and tell people bad things like their kids have been molested by their neighbor and I just act like I'm an anonymous citizen trying to help or I get meaner and tell them I'm going to kill them or their kids. I do it for a laugh because I don't really care about how they feel. I know that and it's just how I am. I've even written an anonymous email to my mother, too, but I think she knows it's me. I wrote telling her that I'm going to kill her son who is a "CUNT" and a "FAGGOT" who doesn't deserve to live. She never wrote back to that email. I guess it's better that she didn't. Anyway today is my birthday and so I'm staying in my room. I duct taped the windows and door closed and am planning on chatting with some people. We'll see how that goes.

XXXIV. INTEGRITY

The door opens and Seth walks in.

"I'm here," he says. "I'm late but I'm here."

The other people in the room nod and open their books. They are ready to learn both from the text and from Seth himself.

HIS WORDS ARE IMPORTANT AND ARE A BASIS FOR A LOT OF THE TEXTS.

Seth starts to speak and for the next several hours his words are imported into the ears of the others in the room, an almost subconscious flow, a subtle but substantial accumulation of knowledge, insight, wisdom, strategies, tactics, plans, logistics, commentary, explanations and even excuses (I HAD TO DO IT OR ELSE I WOULD…) The lecture finally ends and everyone goes to sleep on the floor. Their dreams reflect the gnosis of the reflexive universe expanding beyond the veils, hail, fell swoop, galaxies spirits bodies light recollection and finally alpha omega cicada verbatim verboten ad nauseam. Heads spread yoga style across the spheres, archons out on bail, relocate witness, black van duct tape lubricant bible blue salt.

"You are the weakest people I've ever met."

XXXV. GNANA

If what you say is true, then we have several things to consider such as the moment when we share, when the acts we omit happen in unison, harmony of the corrupt figures that spin the bottle that holds the universe.

You're right.

Maybe I've jumped the gun.

I have no right to expect anyone to come to my defense. In this world (THIS WORLD BE DAMNED) we are all independent beings striving for interdependence. If someone strikes me on the cheek, I must turn and give them my other. I CANNOT EXPECT ANOTHER PERSON TO COME TO MY DEFENSE AND OFFER THEIR OWN CHEEK / IT IS UNFAIR TO ASK ANYONE TO DO THAT / I AM MY OWN MY OWN PERSON

This interdependence…this myth of friendship, brotherhood, closeness of spirit…What a myth it is. The myth of the Demiurge, illusions propped up by weak and crumbling stone thin theater constructed (DECONSTRUCTED) by effeminate jesters who breathe the sullen breath of G-D into the universe. A bloated toad in a garden DON'T EAT THIS

FRUIT OR YOU WILL SUFFER THE CONSEQUENCES…

Consequences? Oh, you ugly toad! So bloated and arrogant, quick to anger, vengeful and jealous. You want our sons. No! You are a brother of Molech and I reject your diagnosis (diaGNOSIS!) and drugs. I am my own man, you bloated toad, and I will stamp the fruit of this garden into dust! Clay! Spit! Breath! I will reinvent myself and my image with NO EXPECTATIONS OF SUCCESS!

You are weak. We are all weak.

XXXVI. PLEROMATIC

As a child, Seth was shy. As an adult, Seth embraces all outward expression: he destroys the boundaries that restrict his gut feelings, the sparks of Christ. HE HAS NO FEAR.

That is not completely true. He fears much. He fears abandonment. He fears being left in the galactic garden of THIS TRASHCAN EARTH.

No one is left. He himself has abandoned all the weak sycophants.

Sets the bomb.

Watches it explode.

All those people are now dust.

XXXVII. ARREST

Voices in the hallway.

"I have nothing to say to you."

"Oh, how about an apology?"

"An apology for what? I didn't do anything wrong."

"That's the point. You never think you do anything wrong. I don't know what to say, man. I love you but for the last few months you've been out of control. You're not the same person. You're…different."

"Bullshit. I can't help if I react to people treating me like shit."

"You're being paranoid."

"And you're being insensitive and judgmental."

"I'm done. I'm tired of dealing with this."

"You're always tired when you have to deal with other people's feelings."

"That's not fair."

"Don't be such a pussy."

"I'm done. I can't handle this. I'm so done. I'm having a panic attack now."

"Leave. Just leave me like the rest of them!"

XXXVIII. TEMPLES

The bomb goes off.... a loud surprise in the high rise. Praising all, the empty spirit, breath of G-D rekindling the fires of new men in a new town, hooks in the eyes of blind messiahs laughing it off in jesters' garb, a redundant tragedy over and over and over.

I don't take joy in this tragedy. I don't take joy in any of it but...

Such is life.

Multiple holocaust survivors reenacting scenes in pornographic fashion. Pedophilia as a history lesson. Videotapes. Preschool panic. In all glory forever and ever and ever. Methamphetamine urge. The urge to snort and shoot and smoke and GOD THIS IS GOOD. GOD IS GOOD. The kid is worth nothing. The kid is worth a few hundred at least. Trade her. Trade her for some GOD THIS IS GOOD SHIT.

The bomb goes off. People die. So what? Limbs everywhere. So what? Blood. So what?

I don't take joy in this tragedy. I don't take joy in any of it but...

Such is life.

XXXIX. CHINESE NEW YEAR

September 26, 2002
November 26, 2002
January 26, 2003
March 7, 2003
September 11, 2004
September 20, 2004
September 30, 2004
November 26, 2004
December 4, 2004
October 12, 2005
May 8, 2006
June 13, 2007
September 13, 2007
May 15, 2007
February 25, 2008
March 3, 2009
March 23, 2010
April 13, 2010
April 28, 2010
April 29, 2010
April 30, 2010
May 12, 2010
August 3, 2010
August 29, 2011
December 14, 2012

HUMANITY IS THE DEVIL

September 9, 2013

XL. MY FAVORITE THINGS

Dissolved temazepam into the tea, said the survivor of Japan Airlines Flight 123.

Girl, 14, accused of stabbing her sister 40 times.

Serial killer Joanna Dennehy takes pictures of herself before stabbing fourth and fifth victims.

HIV-positive college student secretly filmed sex tapes with 23 people.

"If I had a gun right now I'd make you do anything I'd want you to do because all of my life people kept doing that to me. What goes around comes around. It's just a snake eating its tail. I suffered so everyone else has to."

Woman offers Man her infant daughter for sex. Man says he will be filming it. Woman says that's even better but the price goes up. Man agrees. Business transaction is complete.

Amen.

XLI. GREEN SLIDES

The lord, the king, named SLAUGHTER, named so for his royal duties, his royal blood sword, a blade christened by eight-thousand and forty-six decapitations in his previous life. Folklore that prepares for reality, that bastion of mentally ill black magic.

Lord Slaughter, the capitalist of terror, reconciles heaven and earth, splits the atmosphere, creates a piss filled sky and blood earth, bone soil, fault lines splitting puddles magma crater, sinkhole, throwing the young bodies in, serpent scales, weight of flesh cockeyed genitals left in the woods, found by a German shepherd, half eaten, this is the Lord's day, earthquake holocaust.

There are no better days.

In the secluded house, babies thrown into the pit. The mothers don't care. In fact, they got pregnant in order to be able to see their offspring suffer in the hole. The mothers (all of which were raped as children) had no more empathy inside them. That's understandable, isn't it?

Lord Slaughter goes by the name of Dunblane. He used to teach kindergarten. He used to be a father. He used to be a GOOD MAN.

XLII. HYLIC MANIA

Mr. Dunblane's knife (and ONLY his knife) enters the girl. Mr. Dunblane's hand (and ONLY his hand) twists and turns and throbs in and out in and out and all wet, wet, wet. It was easy for Mr. Dunblane to sweet talk the girl online... (I'm a NICE guy) and take advantage of the situation she was in...divorced parents...a dad who only sees her once a week and a mother who is too stressed out to keep a close eye on her daughter's internet activity.

"u r my sweetie," Mr. Dunblane said.

"aww," the girl said.

The knife cuts everything up, cuts her mother's heart out WHERE WERE YOU WHEN THIS WAS HAPPENING? The girl (Mr. Dunblane's doesn't actually remember her name. This ACT has gone beyond a human-to-human relationship) begins to scream much louder...a banshee, a siren, an alarm...

Mr. Dunblane cuts it off at its source, basks in the blood glorious dark relentless, wraps her up in the tarp. Mr. Dunblane's mind recalls the word carp, carp flag, what a gory flag, celebrate kids' day, kids' day indeed. Dumps her somewhere, he doesn't remember. Mr. Dunblane doesn't remember. The comprehensive diagnostic tests show there was no consistent levels of aptitude evident. There is no skill, no ability to reason to what we seek to achieve in our studies and experiments. If there is hope, it is hidden behind a severely impaired exterior.

Zabala shotgun
Browning shotgun
Beretta 92FS semi-automatic 9mm pistol
CZ ORSO semi-automatic .32-caliber pistol
Bernardelli .22-caliber pistol
"Type 56" 7.62x39mm semi-automatic rifle
Hi-Point model 995 carbine rifle
TEC-DC9 9mm semi-automatic handgun
Springfield XD (M) semi-automatic pistol
Ruger MK III semi-automatic handgun

The selective mutism myth.
Autism as a form of empowerment.
Outpatient treatment.
Mental illness as a road to intellectual prowess.

Revenge should be random and majestic.

XLIII. AVANT

The painting in question (labeled INJECTION AND INVOCATION SPIRAL MODERN 134 in most catalogs) remains an enigma but not altogether complex example of the significant influence of the pseudo-Sethian movement on the subsequent phases of the underground art scene of the 1920s. That being said, the painting is widely known mostly as a curio, a novelty artifact reserved for nostalgic kitsch. In fact, most references to it are rather condescending which negate the importance of the work.

XLIV. BLAME

Bomb the ignorant spectators. Destroy them with your mystical cosmology! Lock picker doomsayer, relent repent repeat deceit dissent. I have a very clear memory of climbing out of my crib and falling into a pile of chemical-soaked rags, coughing choking and someone picked me up, slapped me, threw me against the wall, I waited and then I dreamt I think. Sexually abused illegal alien torture video clip download upload teddy bear grasshopper ambulance electroshock masochism sticky feet a special kind of puberty and poverty. Too much trauma to the head. I cannot will not think straight until when. A big man stuck his hand in me, his whole hand.

January, 2014. A 16-year old student sets himself on fire in a Colorado high school. "This is not someone's fault," he said. "I had planned this for years." He survived. "If anyone says that they know why I did this...nobody knows and nobody will."

His whole hand.

XLV. VIOLATED

Seth throws a brick through the stained glass, shattering Christ, pitter patter of mice in the garden, pardon me.

Tooth cloth shroud egg death swallowed. The objective of the third mission is to weaken the Demiurge's infrastructure in the educational system. THIS HAS NOTHING TO DO WITH CHILDREN PARTICULARY IT HAS TO DO WITH TRUTH wisdom knowledge things. What fruit will you expose? What will you sow and reap? Brilliant lies, subtle consequences, mirrored desolation infestation abomination of all 13 entrances…you need to show I.D. before they let you go inside. HEY KIDS. Bring your ID and EGO. I'm surprised you even agreed to this. CAR BOMB. Detonation education. Molestation at the crash site. The worst possible scenario you can imagine, times 7 times 7 times 7. That's the truth you find in the garage, in the closet, in the trunk, in the basement, on file at the local police department, true, deportation, border predators, black out rapist, they called him. Pick axe evisceration, erotic disembowelment, hammer fashion, human landmines, families under attack, bullet holes, violation VIOLATION!

XLVI. SOLO

Falcone drops dead from a heart attack. His mother finds his magazines (LOW DOWN DEATH, SKINNY RUBBER DISORDER, NECROP, STRUCTURES) and his binders full of photographs, mostly Polaroid, as young as 3.

His mother faints, wakes to find:

IT IS NOT A DREAM, SHE DID NOT IMAGINE IT.

She forces herself to look for more PAIN RAPE ABUSE and she finds it, hidden under the bed, in his bowling bag, worse than the other stuff, more in his underwear drawer, with the pages of HARMLESS magazines and books (TRUE CRIME) and in the trunk of his car. If she had known anything about computers she would have found THOUSANDS OF PICTURES AND HUNDREDS OF HOURS OF VIDEO FOOTAGE and it would have SHOCKED HER INTO WANTING TO GO BACK IN TIME AND FOLLOW THROUGH WITH THE ABORTION. KILL THE BABY WHO WILL GROW UP TO ABUSE BABIES.

XLVII. SOMEONE ANYONE

I've killed people. I've done it not in cold blood but in a calculating logical manner, burying my emotional response and looking at things from a strategic perspective, the bigger picture, a means to an end, so yeah I've killed people.

Sometimes I wish I didn't feel so disconnected. A small part of me envies that sort of intimacy that I see (and that I fake). To feel loyalty and love towards another human being... that's so foreign to me but it seems so important to everyone else. I would never die for anyone else. I would never sacrifice for anyone else. But people do it and I'm fascinated at the concept of self-sacrifice.

Most people don't kill. Most people would never kill except under the most extreme circumstances. But I've killed for nothing but curiosity and then, eventually, pleasure. It makes me feel good to be alive at the moment someone is dying. It's actually quite life affirming. I think if more people knew that feeling, there would be a lot more murders. I feel special, though. I'm special. I've killed people and I know how it feels and when I die, when I am killed, I will know how it feels, and the circle will be complete like a snake eating its tail.

XLVIII. RAIL

Seth is naked in the park. He is natural. He thinks himself a snake. He does a cartwheel, he somersaults, he rolls in the grass, eats the grass, chews like the beasts of the field. He is not ill. He is as healthy as ever. His body glows.

Exhausted.

Hallucinatory prefix.

There are no mice in the garden.

Snakes!

Seth eats more grass, his stomach expands, collapses, implodes, neurological cicada white black bicycles. The grass is mowed.

You're lucky I agreed to this.

But I resent you.

Obelisk.

Is it bad if I would derail a train to help the boy?

You'd kill the boy!

I would not.

Does that make me a bad person?

Quality before quantity!

Kamikaze messiah.

Solar sabbat.

I will block out the sun with my stomach pains.

You're not a good father.

XLIX. AMERICANA

Perpetual penetration our sister of fortitude. In praise of a broken foot. The perpetrators entered the residence and beat the occupants with lead pipes and committed sodomy. No number of stitches will heal the desecrated cavities, in through the out door, tight and reluctant, no, terrified girls. Circle of menstrual blood, a flood, barely breathing seraphim within the wheel and hemorrhaging ceremonies.

Falcone's father disappeared in Argentina back in the 1970s. Could he be one of the bloated bodies? (BLOATED TOAD!) Maybe. Falcone thinks so and he worshipped a photograph for years.

Hail BLOATED DISSIDENT.

This is a hand grenade. May I have another glass of sparkling water? My throat is parched and I'm remembering memories of recollection of nostalgia of circumference of clouds, ha, forget the schoolgirl death pose, perfume ejaculate, sex offender registry death squad. Relaxed colon, flippant attitude, flipped off the judge, jerk off gesture, jerk off instruction, pet names for private parts, pigtails and lye, wet cement, braces. Poured gasoline on the witnesses, kills their kids, whatever. Posted it on the internet, pictures, crime scene blasphemy avant garde kink exploring the relationship between human rights and elitist pleasure. The 120 days of Florida. Mark Karr solicited the undercover officer over the internet. Dresses as a woman, breaks hearts like a man. Four minute internet clip of a man breaking a child in half. You should read the comments. Some of them are hilarious. You should see that other video. The one with the woman gagging while two cocks compete for a path down her ugly gullet. I think the woman died by the end of the video. I don't know. Her eyes are all bulging and she doesn't move. The men slap her a few times, spit on her, and then just laugh and leave her there and the camera just lingers on her for a few seconds, zooms in on her spit/cum/drool/vomit covered face and then FADES TO BLACK.

L. LESSONS & LIARS

Seth thinks about eschatology.

Who is Antichrist?

He hasn't heard a theory he liked.

Who is Antichrist?

Perhaps the Demiurge himself.

Perhaps the corrupted, the perverted, the inverted seraphim born from Lilith's infected wound, that slithering cunt of hers, gaping agony, a piss poor example of motherhood, of a child snatcher. Her haven in Edom, her face flushed red with queen's blood, spilled into the carpet, coffee maker, splendor of the gas suffocating a room full of infants to appease who? It's a shame about Doeg, for sure. He is responsible for the liars.

LI. A DRILL

White flags fill the windows. ONE DEAD THREE WOUNDED

Blood spots, sun spots, sun blood. Let's all agree that the destruction of the "temple" is a positive step towards the reconciliation of WHATEVER. That's it, we start, we block the firmament with our bodies of light. BUT WE ARE TRULY NOT SO CLEVER.

I am offering you a chance of a lifetime. You will make the most out of your life if you shed all hope of salvation, this corrupt shell, and you are but a sickly and bloated toad.

The students have been sacrificed. They will never go to college, no, but we've learned a valuable lesson and they are looking down on us.

TWO DEAD THREE WOUNDED.

We are not so clever. We've never been. We pretend to be so clever. We pretend to know all the secrets and the answers to the riddles but we're idiots. I'm okay with that. I'm just an idiot. I'm a moron. I'm borderline mentally ill. I'm waving the white flag.

THREE DEAD THREE WOUNDED.

LII. DITZY SCENE

Enough of this funny business, enough of this posturing. We must take real action. We must plant the seeds of our sparks (the sparks of our seed) and hope for the rain of splendor, of incorruptible solutions to the problem of OUR BODIES AND HOW THEY BETRAY US IN EVERY WAY SHAPE AND FORM AND VOID AND SUBSTANCE.

Poor excuse for a weakling. Poor excuse for a BODY and FORM AND VOID in the firmament. I have nothing to say to you. (You have nothing to say to yourself!)

I sent you a letter but you didn't respond. DID I CONFESS TOO MUCH?

I've always been TOO HONEST and now I think I've had TOO MUCH to drink. Not drunk, really but just…OUT THERE.

LIII. LIGHTS CAMERA

Seth pulls a gun ("I was never really a fan of guns.") and fires a shot that shatters a window and wounds a 34 year old father of three. ("I don't think I ever want children.") He fires another shot and it ricochets off a metal rail, speeding in the direction of an elderly woman and her head pops. ("Sometimes I wish I had known my grandparents.") Sirens alert Seth to trouble. He runs around the side of the building and pulls out his cell phone. ("I've always been a bit of a Luddite but I've given in to technology.") He calls his unofficial second-in-command and updates him on the action. ("Action is an art form in and of itself.")

LIV. EAST

As far as I could tell, the guy was shooting randomly into the crowd, just moving the gun back and forth and firing. Luckily I was standing on the other side of the store but I wasn't going to stay and wait for him so I ran. All I could think about was my wife and how she didn't know where the hell I was so if she saw the shooting on the news she would have no idea that I was there. That scared me a lot.

I heard him yell something. I don't really remember his exact words but it was something about fire or sparks or flames. I don't know. He was shouting but he also sort of sounded calm.

I would have tried to save some of the people but I just couldn't move. I guess I was in shock. But also I think I've always been one to avoid confrontation be it verbal or physical and I just couldn't bring myself to go up there and try to save those people.

LV. WEST

One second he was holding my hand and the next minute I felt nothing. My hand wasn't attached to him anymore. My son was gone. People were screaming. The air was grey and then purple like a veil covering the other side of the mall and then there was a huge boom that knocked me to the floor and I fell onto something that squeaked and then cracked.

LVI. NORTH AND SOUTH

Where's my son? Has anyone seen my son?
What does he look like?
Brown hair…he's only six years old.
What is he wearing?
I…I don't remember.
Think. What was he wearing?
A blue shirt, I think. Jeans, too, I think.
Where was he?
He was holding my hand?
Then what?
He was gone.
Is that him?
Where?
There.
No.
Is that him?
No.
How tall is he?
I don't know…uh…average.
Is that him?
No.
How old is he?
He's six.
Is that him?
No.

What color is his hair?

Brown.

I think I saw a little boy a minute ago. He was running that way.

Was it my son?

I don't know.

What was he wearing?

I don't remember.

Can you help me?

What's his name?

LVII. STONES

The ability to change the social environment is gained by…by what?

We don't know.

Who knows?

No one knows.

The amount of time invested in this, some spectacular display of complex reconstruction of our surroundings. We blow through our cash and gather supplies. Not all power comes from political connections, you know. There is power of fire. The power of terrifying brute force. The traumatizing of the innocents (as if there are really any INNOCENTS). Terror is the nucleus of our plan for the dismantling of the archfiend's (Demiurge's) manipulative structure, this holographic dungeon, this vile orb hidden behind a vile veil. Ammunition and explosive pornography. The last stand of the millennium.

He who has no sin…

LVIII. PLANS

Seth stands on the corner of Washington Road and Harrison Street.

Nondescript man.

Armed man.

The Amboy Bank is right across the street.

Small building. Last remodeled in 1999.

Think about it.

Go in there.

Shoot the first few people you see.

STRIKE FEAR.

Find an elderly employee, slit her throat, jack off with the blood.

SHOW THEM YOU MEAN BUSINESS. STRIKE FIRST STRIKE FEAR. NO MERCY GIVEN NO MERCY EXPECTED.

Make them sing.

G-D BLESS AMERICA MY HOME SWEET HOME INVASION.

LIX. RANDOM ACTS OF KINDNESS

I am fat. I am ugly. I am a poor example of a MAN. How did I get like this? Where did the time go? HOW MANY YEARS HAVE I BEEN ASLEEP AT THE WHEEL? There's only one way to STRIKE FEAR STRIKE BACK STRIKE UP A CONVERSATION WITH all those nice people around me who probably don't notice how FAT AND UGLY I am but I'll still resent them and expect them to say SOMETHING ANYTHING to me about what I look like. What am I supposed to do? HOW DID I GET THIS GUT? How did I get this gun? I'M A POOR EXAMPLE OF A MAN. I am a poor example of a human being. I'M ASLEEP AT THE WHEEL.

I'm not that bad looking.
WHERE IS MY REVENGE?

LX. FRIENDSHIP SCHEME

There is no force worth using other than BRUTE FORCE so in one swift motion (one planned aktion-bruit) you can destroy the hope that festers in the hearts of those unprepared, unenlightened, unexposed to the truth, light, dreams long dead, an utter excuse of mania, an utterance to break the bond between MEDIA REPORTS and recorded footage REAL TIME STAMP OUT RAGE SHOOTER with trembling tongues of customers hiding within clothing racks (lingerie blood splatter tragic exposure sirens in the background) and so on. I shot the cunts execution style, raped and violated the angels like a kamikaze storm ritual. I would like to know your opinion on the matter because YOUR OPINION IS VERY IMPORTANT TO ME IN THE SCHEME OF THINGS.

LXI. ANYONE

I'm not gonna lie to you, man. I've always been truthful, right, and so I'm always pretty real with you and so basically if I tell you something you can count on it being true. I'm telling you I'm sick and fucking tired of going to work and dealing with this shit. My ex-wife is leaving messages for my boss telling him I have AIDS and that I like to cut myself on purpose and sprinkle the blood all around. Such bullshit, you know, I mean I haven't cut myself in years but she's trying to ruin my life, that bitch, I swear to god. My life is turning to shit as if it could get any worse, right? I'm telling you, man, I'm at the end of my rope. I'm totally going to explode, go out of my head. I'm scaring myself and I guess I'm telling you this so maybe you can help but I don't know if you or anyone could really help. Anyway, give me a call when you get this message.

LXII. ARCHLILIT

Seth is standing on a cliff.

He is looking out at the dust devils (DJINN) and is reciting the Coptic cell phone numbers into the wind. Nothing happens. Nothing will ever happen. This is the geometry of Ba'al surrounded by algebraic flies.

No type of spell can counteract progress.

THERE IS NO GOD BUT ONE GOD ONLY GOD ONE GOD.

Seth views the horizon as the bottom of the glass dome that has captured all the evil in the world. He must bring it down. He wants to rape the world in a fiery display of POWER POWER POWER and revenge.

LXIII. FRIENDSHIP SCHEME II

Intricate plans to escape from the grasp of the EVIL BOSS, the epitome of insobriety of spirit, OH HIS TEMPER, setting fire to his temple. If I have to drive all over for this, I expect something in return. I have your home address. I have everything I need. I have guns. I have guns and I have dynamite. I have a hell of a lot of weapons to fight and I'll fight. I'll fight. PICK UP YOUR PHONE.

LXIV. EXPLANATION

Splatter tome refinished basement packages televisions chairs electronic blots blemishes faces crinkled mirrors scorpions antiques ordered reordered gunshots daycare abusing diaper rabbi slot pillow online electro-disease as head of the air force plastic torture genital photographs neurotten surgery pain labs take my meds

LXV. POLLY POCKET

Splendor tone refurnished backlit smacks telephones chains electrical blips blessings traces wrinkled dearest scorpio anthems bordered snorted abuse air torture surgery blocks soup subtlety laugh flux paid worker ugly gash spotlight steaming shit streaming video ordered televised chairs something truthful some mother slit her daughter's throat because a guy on the internet said it'd turn him on.

LXVI. WEAKNESSES

Voices on the computer.

"I'm tired of you yelling at people."

"Yelling? How was I yelling?"

"You were yelling and cursing at him. I'm sick of it."

"He deserved it."

"Did he? Really? Give me a break."

"You don't even know the whole story."

"I know enough."

"No, you don't. You don't know shit. Why do you choose now to take sides? Whenever I have a problem and I want your support, you stay neutral but now you're taking sides. What the hell is wrong with you?"

"There's nothing wrong with me. I'm just sick of you."

"I guess I'll leave you alone."

LXVII. FROZEN

Where's my son?

I DON'T KNOW ANYTHING ABOUT YOUR SON.

He was just here.

I DIDN'T SEE ANYONE.

He was standing right here. Right next to you.

I DIDN'T SEE ANY KID. I DIDN'T SEE ANYONE.

I saw him. He was standing right next to you. How could you not see him?

I DIDN'T SEE HIM. I DIDN'T SEE ANYONE.

He has brown hair. He was wearing a t-shirt with a monster truck on it.

I DIDN'T SEE HIS SHIRT. I DIDN'T SEE HIM. I DIDN'T SEE ANYONE.

Where's my son? I'm serious. Where is he? I just turned around for a second.

I DIDN'T SEE ANYONE. I DON'T KNOW WHERE YOUR SON IS.

He's six years old. He was just here. I saw him. He was standing right next to you.

I DIDN'T SEE ANYONE.

How could you not see him? He was standing right next to you.

HUMANITY IS THE DEVIL

I DON'T KNOW ANYTHING ABOUT YOUR SON.

LXVIII. AMERICANA II

The video starts abruptly: a living room, plastic sheets, family photos on the walls MOM DAD TWO KIDS NORMAL SMILING and a man enters, not the same man in the picture, NOT THE FATHER, but A MAN NONETHELESS. He is dragging a woman. She has a PLASTIC BAG over her head. She is otherwise naked. The man grabs her throat. "Got a surprise for you," he says. He slaps her. He squeezes her throat. He rips the bag off her head. Her face is DEEP DEEP DEEP red. The man masturbates with his other hand. Ejaculates into her mouth. Lets go of her throat so she could swallow. "I have AIDS," he says. "Stupid cunt."

MOVIE OVER.

The rest of the tape is blank.

LXIX. BEST LAID

I'm letting you off the hook this time because I think you have potential.

That's what Seth said to me. I was reluctant to believe him, obviously. I never thought I ever had potential for anything. I'm pretty average, unassuming, unremarkable, a typical man, a typical human being, a typical thing. That's my situation and I am content, I think, in that position. So, Seth said this to me and I scoffed but I found myself planting an explosive in a shopping mall.

LXX. TENSION

Akutagawa puffed on his cigarette. "I don't want anything to do with this."

Mr. Dunblane smiled. "But you haven't heard everything."

"I don't need to. I don't want anything to do with it."

"Don't be a fool, Akutagawa."

"Who are you kidding? I've always been a fool. I've never had any problem with that."

"That's going to be the death of you."

"So be it, Mr. Dunblane. I'm gonna go now."

"I'll walk with you."

"No. I'm going alone."

"The hell you are, Akutagawa."

"Have it your way."

"As always." Mr. Dunblane smiles, takes the cigarette out of Akutagawa's mouth, and puts it into his own.

LXXI. DOME DREAMS

Last night a young woman's body was found outside her home in Rochester. She may have been sexually assaulted. Police are still investigating but say they don't have any leads.

Last night campus police found several copies of a pamphlet strewn on the floor of the university library. The pamphlet, *HOW TO DESTROY YOUR FRIENDS*, is suspected to have originated from one of the many clandestine student clubs which, as you may remember, were banned last semester.

Last night I slept in a box behind the Amboy Bank. It was cold. I used a tarp as a blanket. I fell asleep to memories of pornographic magazines I had masturbated to in the past.

LXXII. AND SO ON

Seth is a man who knows his stuff.

He won't turn the gun on himself.

No.

That's not an option.

Martyrdom, that's one thing, but suicide, no way, that's not a choice Seth believes in. It is nonexistent in his destiny, his fate, or the weak foundation of all outcomes for every decision he has made thus far.

Seth shot several people.

A few of them were women. One was a man. Two were children. It was *basically* random. They were right there after the first blast went off and Seth needed to clear the way. He needed to send a message. He needed to spark things into existence if that's even possible.

Sometimes he doubts his plan, his own motives, his own path, but he still goes about his business because what's the point of waking up today if you aren't going to follow through with what you started yesterday?

And so on.

LXXIII. POSTAGE

Early in the morning (before the EVENT), Seth sent nine postcards to various government offices. On those postcards were words, not exactly threats, but as close as you can get to threats without actually being threatening.

Here I am who exists as son for ever and ever.

Don't count us out yet.

You are what you are, you are who you are.

The sun is shining, the son is shining, your sons are missing.

Here's an aeon for you!

Tell Barbelo WE said hello.

The emanations you WILL see will BLIND you. Sleep tight.

The serpent with the lion's head chews YOUR YOUNG.

WITH laughter, we will DELIGHT in the demise of the craftsman.

LXXIV. BLAME

There's something wrong with me.

I fell for it.

I fell for his tricks.

Yeah, I'm pretty sure they're tricks.

Just tricks.

Words implanted somewhere (in my head??) and transmitted, too, voices no one can hear or will not hear but I do (like saying, THE GREAT BEAST KING HAS SWALLOWED THE BLOOD SWORD OF VENGEANCE IN THE REALM OF THE UNBEGOTTEN LIGHT) and there's no escaping from it.

I have a gun.

I have dynamite.

I have my orders.

I have to do it. I have a lot of things I need to do. Public safety will be a myth. THERE WILL BE NOTHING LEFT of your security. SO WHAT? SO WHAT NOW? Your world is corrupt, I think. Maybe. But maybe I just fell for THE OLDEST TRICK IN THE BOOK. TRICKS, THEY WERE ALL TRICKS.

What are you talking about?

EVEN THEIR LOGOS ARE TRICKS OF THE GREAT SETH EMBLAZONED ON THEIR JACKETS.

LXXV. HOW TO RAISE FLOWER BULBS

Her guts were piping hot.
So good were her guts.
So virginal were her guts.
Her guts were piping hot.
So good were her guts.
So virginal were her guts.
So pure.
So pure were her guts.
Horoshi Suzuki, the blackened face of my desire. Somewhere between love and orgasm is terror and that is my favorite part. She played in the park. I watched. I watched her play in the park. Swing, little thing, swing.
Her guts were piping hot.
So pure.
So good, so good, that blackened face of my despair.
I played in the park.
I ran around.
I watched her.
I watched her swing. Somewhere between her guts and her beauty is the pinnacle of my arousal, piping hot and pure as snow.
So pure.

LXXVI. GOOD KID

After months of mourning, the mother finally enters her son's bedroom.

It looks the same, sort of, but she notices a stillness that was never there before. She realizes she's being ridiculous. The reason is obvious. Her son had cleaned the room before he left for school. It was the last chore he had done, one last expression to let his mother know he cared.

The mother sits on the bed for a while, crying just a little bit, not like before. She caresses the pillow. She turns on the lamp on the night stand. She opens up the drawer and rummages through: music magazines, scraps of notebook paper, a broken cigarette, a pocket knife, a cassette tape (labeled *Study of Joy in Blood and Torture Hell*), a pack of matches, a comic book (AIM-AUM), candy wrappers. Underneath it all, the mother finds a manila folder which she slowly opens.

LXXVII. MISSED

Photos printed out from the computer.

A woman wrapped mummy-like in plastic wrap…each eye covered with an X made of duct tape. Her breasts are exposed and tied with ropes…they are on the verge of exploding. There is only a small dime-sized hole over the woman's mouth. There is a caption under the picture written in her son's handwriting: SLUTS GET WHAT THEY DESERVE LOL!

Another photo: a naked man kneeling over an eviscerated cat. The man's face is blurred.

Next: a black and white photo of a pile of bodies, causalities of war.

Men, women, and children.

Half-naked.

Shot, mutilated.

Some disemboweled.

Soldiers nearby smiling, guns up in the air, obviously satisfied with their work.

The mother is barely able to look at the last picture.

It is her son holding a gun to an infant's head. The baby is crying. Her son is smiling. In his fourteen years alive, he had never smiled so wide.

The mother drops the photos to the ground and collapses to the floor.

LXXVIII. KISSING MR. DUNBLANE

"In a way," said **Mr. Dunblane,** "I respect what you did, standing up to me like that. I mean, not many people would do that and you're the last person I'd expect. That being said, I'm still pissed off and you're still going to have to pay. That's just the way it is. Think of it as a matter of honor. I'd hate to say this but it's really your fault. If you had been consistent with your behavior, with your actions, then you wouldn't have gotten into this situation to begin with. But you chose the wrong time to grow a backbone and try to be a man. You never were good with being a man, you know? I'm not criticizing you, just stating a fact. In a way you were a breath of fresh air but then you had to fuck it up by doing what you did and now you have to take what's coming to you, you know?"

LXXIX. TWO DOWN

Seth thinks the words sound nice. The rhythm, the entire structure…everything about the sentence signified what he wanted to express with guttural yet gorgeous wordplay. He looks at the postcard one last time and puts it into the mailbox.

Now he'll wait.

He doesn't like waiting.

Then again, who does?

He's waited all his life, really. He's waited for things to *happen*.

Sure, he tries to make those things happen but a lot of it is out of his control.

He knows this.

He accepts this.

He waits.

The words reverberate through his brain and turn into physical vibrations through his muscles, bones, and nerves. He has the urge to run.

He doesn't run.

He waits.

LXXX. INTERLUDE

A MAN STUDYING THE REMAINS OF THE BLACK PSYCHOMANTEUM

Black words on black paper:
Hell on/is EARTH...
Zoom in on girl's face (No older than 6).

FAINT GLOW.

Adult male enters scene to the sound of CHIMES (OR GONGS).

"May I be of assistance?"

"I want to go home."

"We all do, honey. We all do."

WHY IS HER FACE MADE OF OBSIDIAN?

Christ is my favorite character.

He says, *"You broke the vile veil."*

LXXXI. DANIEL

I don't like going to my therapist. I don't think he knows what my real problems are. I talk to him but I don't tell him everything, obviously, because I don't want to get into trouble. I just tell him maybe half of my issues and I feel weird holding back but I know I can't tell him everything. He just sort of sits there, listens, and asks some questions but I don't think he actually cares or understands not that I can blame him. I can't imagine having to listen to other people's problems all day every day. That sounds like torture. It's not his fault I'm messed up but I still don't like going. My parents make me go and there's nothing I can really do about it. I know they wouldn't let me even leave the house if I didn't agree to see him so that's the situation I'm in now.

LXXXII. SYMPATHY

The boy walks into the school.
He shoots.
He scores.
He's ahead of the game.
His game plan.
Hit a teacher or two.
Pull the fire alarm.
Ducks in a barrel.
Get as many as he can.
Rack up the points.
Wishes he could see all the parents' faces.
So long.
You'll never understand me.

LXXXIII. FRIENDS ARE EVIL

Every person I know personally is on some form of antidepressant or has been at one time or another and/or goes to therapy. Quite a few have been institutionalized at some point in their lives. Am I a magnet for people like this? For people like myself? Or is everyone just as damaged as I am?

If I had wanted to, could I have found someone who would have joined me in my "rampage"? Maybe. But I have always been shy and reluctant to share my desires, my dreams, and the sources of my anger, my despair. If I had confided in someone, would they have turned me in or would they have joyfully taken part in my plans? Would anyone have understood my situation? No, probably not.

I don't blame anyone else. Not even Steven. Not even him despite the...attention he paid me as a child (from when I was 7 to about 13). I started out hating him but began to expect it all and find comfort in the abuse. I don't blame him for anything. What happened, happened. I can't go back in time and stop him from violating me in all those different ways. He taught me things I certainly had no business knowing, not at that age. Not ever, really.

So that's it. Why did I do the things I did? No one, not even me, will ever know.

LXXXIV. SIMPLE NONSENSE

There's no problem with what I do. I choose to do it. I make a conscious decision to do it. And them? Oh, they're just collateral damage. I'm tired of talking about it. Let's move on...

Is this world a hologram? A mirrored shell? Maybe. So really whatever happens inside it doesn't really "happen"...it's like a reflection of a shadow in a dream...That's the best I can describe it. This world is actually constructed quite poorly. The architect didn't do a thorough job in building something permanent, stable, meaningful. The architect is like an autistic madman with a near infinite supply of building blocks, mere toys compared to the real fabric of reality. If you look hard enough, you can see the glitches. Actually they are not difficult to see at all. What am I seeing? See this here...One glitch.

Read the news. Every meaningless rape, murder, act of torture, genocide, child abuse, and so on and so forth...

I yearn for the sparks. I yearn for the sparks that will illuminate the real world and set this illusionary one on fire but then again...What will really burn? What will be consumed by the flames?

LXXXV. WARNING SIGNS

You can blame violent video games, heavy metal music, and shoot-em-up movies and perhaps even the medication the defendant was on (in this case Taborica)…but it's mental illness, a lapse in his ability to perceive reality as it really is. This could not be helped. No one, especially the defendant, would have prevented this tragedy. It was set in motion sixteen years ago, when he was conceived. It is a result of, dare I say, "bad biology"…a genetic glitch that caused his brain to become ill while he was still in his mother's womb. We can't possibly know for sure how early the warning signs became evident. It's obviously saddening that the defendant's parents were also victims of this tragedy. But remember this is a result of illness. We don't arrest those who have colds. We don't arrest those who happen to sneeze on another person. The ill person can only take so many precautions but there's a limit and after a certain extent, the illness is in charge and there's no stopping it. There was no stopping this. You can only blame the illness.

LXXXVI. IDOLS

Voices on the phone.

"You wanna come with me tomorrow?"

"Where?"

"I'm gonna go shoot some kids."

(Laughs) "What are you talking about?"

"I'm going up to the elementary school tomorrow. Gonna shoot some kids in the morning."

"Why?"

"I don't know. Seems like fun. They're always running around, being loud, acting stupid. Whenever I see them I just want to spray those little fuckers with bullets."

(Laughs) "What time?"

"Eight."

"Where?"

"Meet me at the corner and then we'll go into the woods behind the schoolyard."

"Cool."

"This is gonna be fucking great! I can't wait to see those fuckers drop."

(Laughs) "Me too."

LXXXVII. BLOG

Cum bitch burping cunts in a cardboard box lit on fire eating garbage dump menstrual chunks raped by AIDS infected fathers brothers shit on green brown feces sludge lactation strangulation child services illumination genital bruise rash fuck panic memories insertion playroom cookies who wants cookies who wants suck dry celebrate birthday penetration sirens tunnels rocking chair horse stuffed giraffe lock spree smothering cunt forced black crowbar teeth hairless blood plead not guilty suitcase child malnutrition nazi nigger faggot blowtorch porno magazines preschool digital camera defendant history of abuse felony mischief toy box hair box squeezing digital penetration excuses excuses excuses alcoholism drug abuse methadone myth blown out asshole fifty dollars cash crack rock gutter spunk devil worship cock wino elder abuse bed sores roach infested cleavage birthday cake covered in tears excuses in parenting he was such a good kid growing up I don't know why he did what he did but he'll always be our son so we love him love him love him bury the bodies behind trailers burn the cunts in dump the sunshine

LXXXVIII. HOMOSEXUAL RAPE VIDEOS

Members Area

"Fuck him into fragments."

"I'm trying."

"Give it to him. Fuck that fucking bitch."

"Worthless whore."

"Pathetic little cunt."

"Damn, look at his ass."

"Totally destroyed!"

"Fucking faggot. Fucking dirty little faggot."

"Wreck that bitch."

"Faggot!"

"Boy cunt."

"Fuck toy… You're my little fuck toy, right? You dirty piece of faggot shit. Open that shit up for me. Open it! Open your mouth. Can you taste your own shit? Eat your shit off my dick, faggot."

"Fuck him into fragments, man!"

"I'M TRYING."

"Drop that fuckin' load."

Membership $29.95 for 30 days.

LXXXIX. CLIMAX IN COLOR

Bob Moor writes books about violent revolutions. Blood, guts, visceral reactions to conflict and all that.

Rape as a political expression.

Rape as the poor man's vote. All colors or no colors.

Jehovah's apparent inability to settle things out of court. A little infamy isn't a bad thing.

Lucifer objects, throws a fit.

Jesus fingers his holes, slams his gavel. He's on the wrong side.

Bob Moor retreats to his home on Staten Island. He uses a 16mm camera to make film versions of his books. He hires local drug addicts to play the roles. There's never any quiet on the set. That's fine. All things happen for a reason and Moor knows less than the average filmmaker. He giggles while he films.

Bob Moor comforts the homeless and wretched man named David Bunting. Bunting claims to be the real Jehovah, the angry taskmaster. Moor does not believe him but has no reason *not* to believe him.

Why not?

Why can't Bunting be telling the truth?

During the storm called Inez, the cast of Bob Moor's film huddles in the basement.

Bunting says, "It is the *performance* of the perversion that's the problem." The storm subsides. Bob Moor films the cast as they walk outside and bask in the beauty of the post-storm destruction.

XC. DRESS UP

Jerome Brudos receives another catalog in the mail. It is a catalog for women's shoes: *Nachts, wenn der Teufal kam 1998.*

Both his parents died of syphilis when he was an infant.

He has too many headaches. The catalogs help.

He remembers wearing socks on his hands. He didn't want to leave fingerprints.

Strangulation.

Rape after death.

Mutilation.

More rape.

Page 65.

Seminal guilt.

More headaches.

As a child, Jerome witnessed a car accident: a young Boy Scout mangled under a truck tire and nearly flattened. Sexually arousing. Reliving the events.

Watch the little boys cross the road.

Jerome is dressed as an old woman.

Lures them. "Come here and I'll show you..."

Flipping through the catalog, Jerome sees a shoe model that catches his eye in more than the usual way. Her ankle reminds him of his mother's. Her calf reminds him of his aunt's. The shoe is inconsequential. He masturbates to the thought of being stomped to death like an insect.

His mother saying, "Come here and I'll show you…"

The truck tire smashing his testicles.

Bugs Bunny on the television.

Soap in his mouth.

Another headache.

Mommy.

XCI. TO SON

I was standing in the hallway, I remember...

It was the center of the house that was surrounded by several doors (basement, my room, my sister's room, the closet, and the bathroom) as well as the doorway to the kitchen and the dining room. It was in the dining that it happened. My mom was sitting at the dining room table. My father was standing. He was screaming, pointing his finger in her face, slamming his palm down on the table, enraged like usual. And then... and then his hands went around her neck.

That's when my memory cuts out. I don't remember what happened after that. My mom's still alive. She's still married to my father. I don't know what happened.

That's all I remember.

XCII. PARTY ANIMALS

He attends those parties. He chases bugs. He finds it more arousing, more intellectually stimulating, if he swallows the possibly-infected semen rather than let it soak into the lining of his bowels.

"I want the gift. I want the disease. I want to take the road to that blessing…"

"Take my fucking cum, honey," he says. "Take it into your ass."

"Oh yes," the other man says. "I want it. Give me your gift."

XCIII. RIPPER RAPE SURVIVORS

Frans du Toit and Theuns Kruger baking cookies to give out to the children in the neighborhood.

The perfect mass.

Norea is in the bathroom. Duct taped.

Norea thinks.

She thinks: I will be raped and disemboweled. I will be left on the side of a rural road. I will be found barely alive. That is what Norea thinks.

Frans and Theuns masturbate onto the cookies.

Frosting.

They remember their own abuse.

Frans thinks: I was raped by my father when I was just three.

Theuns thinks: My mother let her boyfriend fuck me.

They all think: What did I do to deserve this?

Nothing.

Nothing.

Nothing.

That's the point.

XCIV. HYPOSTASIS OF THE ARCHONS

Drug traffickers, mind control, former Nazis, conservative Christianity, dissociative identity disorder, orgies at car washes, airports, experts, underground pornography, credible witnesses, claims, therapists, anatomically correct dolls, drug barons and child pornographers, televisions, pedophile rings, frivolous rape, fewer cases of abuse confirmed, balloon parties, black vans, trauma to the body. He left with the child. I don't remember what he looks like.

XCV. CRASH AT AN UNKNOWN SPEED

Seth speeds through the intersection.

Will a cop stop him?

Maybe.

Does it matter?

Not really.

If a cop is stupid enough to catch him…then all bets are off. Seth will show the officer his license along with a six-inch gold blade which will go into the pig's throat. (What about the police officer's family?) So what? We all have family in one form or another. No family is better than another. No family is worth more than another. (But he has kids!) So what? Maybe now they won't grow up to be pigs like their father.

Seth slows the car just a bit as he rounds a corner. The tires just barely leave the ground. He lights a cigarette. He blows smoke up towards the windshield. It's like driving through a fog AND HE LIKES THAT, MAN, HE REALLY LIKES THAT.

XCVI. SWORD & SORCERY

Seth uses his sword to disembowel the king. Guts in the throne room. Intestines for the queen, for the jester, for the prince, the little prince.

"Here is your king," Seth shouts, holding up the sword he calls SOPHIASLAYER, the sword he forged himself in the western lands while he lived with a tribe of barbarians, those wretched cunts of the abyss, those cannibals who think nothing of smothering their own infants and eating their brains in the moonlight. Yes, those ugly tribal horrors!

"Here is your king!" Seth shatters skulls. "And here is my holocaust! It begins!"

Internet connection lost.

XCVII. STUDYING RITUAL CRIME

Trouble in the mobile home park.
Steven's Mobile Home Park.
Route Eighteen.
East Brunswick.

Mother, 43, four hundred pounds, dirty, filthy, eighth-grade education, foster kids, web cam, child pornography.

Her boyfriend, 35, one hundred thirty pounds, meth addict, registered sex offender, amateur actor in films, loves to be the star, loves to please and be pleased.

What do the neighbors know?

"Nothin' really. They were good folks. Kept to themselves mostly. Nice people. Never saw nothin' strange."

Kid on a leash eating dog food and raped raw.

"They were good folks. Went to church."

Lots of strange artifacts. Books on the occult. Black candles. Satanic/Nazi pornography found on the computer. War crime magazines under the bed.

XCVIII. ACCURATE ACCOUNT

Who was abused?
Was anyone abused for real?
Yelling is not abuse.
A little spanking is not abuse either.
Was anyone actually abused?
Did anyone have an accident?
A bathroom accident, I mean.
Did anyone touch them inappropriately?
Do I have to define that word? Inappropriately?
Who was abused? Names. I need names.
Was anyone actually abused?
Is it possible that it was self-inflicted?
Children that age sometimes experiment.
Who was abused?
Was someone actually abused?
Were any of them actually abused?
What kind of injuries?
Internal injuries?
What kind of internal injuries?
Could they have been self-inflicted?
Could they have been accidental?
Who was abused?
Who was actually abused?
Were any of them abused?

PART TWO

"And as with all things, by its fruits shall ye know humanity. And humanity's fruits are foul; bruised and bitter, and rotten to the core. And humanity's home is the earth, and the earth is Hell."

– The Process Church of the Final Judgment

HUMANITY IS THE DEVIL

I. SETH

Seth sits in the car.
Exhausted.
Busy day.
So much has been done.
Accomplished.
There were deaths, yeah.
Seth doesn't think of them as simple deaths.
He doesn't think of them as tragedies.
His attacks were not random.
My attacks were not random.
No attack is really random.
Seth turns on the radio.
White noise.
Pink noise.
He wipes dust from the dashboard.
Leaves his fingerprints.
He ponders the idea of being a criminal.
He wonders.
Am I a criminal?
Am I practicing the black art of crime?
Am I a magician of illegality?
White noise.
Pink noise.
He thinks of death.
Dead men.

HUMANITY IS THE DEVIL

Dead women.
Dead kids.
He had wasted them all.
He's snuffed them out.
He's witnessed suffering.
Torture.
Sadism.
That wide-eyed confusion before death.
For a purpose.
There is a purpose to it all, he knows that.
A spark to light the world on fire.
To spite the Demiurge.
Damn the archons.
This is the place.
This is the time.
The moment.
White noise.
Pink noise.
Am I a criminal?

II. HOPES

Friday night at the shopping mall.

That guy, early 40s, black hair, clean shaven, wearing jeans and hooded sweatshirt. Caucasian. Snatched that kid right up. Took his hand, told him to come on, and the kid listened because… why not?

The man brought the kid into the men's restroom on the second floor. The restroom is located down a secluded hallway. Terrible location. The security cameras are working but there is no one watching the live footage.

The kid gets abused in the bathroom. The man cuts the kids hair. Dyes it with spray-on color. Changes the kid into clothes he had stolen. Walks out with the kid.

Two weeks later the body is found.

Raped, strangled.

The parents' prayers went unanswered. But, let's face it: the little kid is in a better place.

That guy, early 40s, black hair, clean shaven, wearing jeans and a hooded sweatshirt (now stained with semen and blood) drives out of state to go move into his mother's house. He's a good son.

III. DREAMS

This flawed creation.

The harmonious universe is a myth. It's crumbling, destroying itself, raping itself, violating itself in so many transcendent ways. The imperfection of the world is something we should all recognize after we get over the initial shock that comes from realizing that no one is really good, nothing is really true, nothing is really right in the world.

Suffering is unavoidable and the sooner one realizes that, the sooner one is able to return to the natural state of apathy. We are flawed. We know fear and pain in the womb. We fear imperfection. We fear pain. We fear our natural state. This hope of some sort of harmony, some sort of benign state of the universe, it's just the dream of a starving soul.

There is a G-D. There is an ultimate, transcendent essence that emanated all things. He is not a creator. He is not a lord and ruler. He is nothing, really. Our apathy suits Him just fine. We can be apathetic about our own essence which is, in essence, the essence of Him.

But down the ladder of existence, we have lost some form of divinity. This is obvious. Look at us.

It doesn't take much intelligence to see that what we are, what we've evolved into is something so sub par in relation to the rest of the features of the realm. Our light is not limitless. Our light is corrupted. It is a camera flash in the basement of a child pornographer. It is a knife blade reflecting the streetlight before it slices across a throat. Can you really say you are proud of this light, this little light of yours? Are you going to let it shine?

Humanity was carved out of nothingness. *That* we cannot reject. But the nothingness, that lack-of-being that has incorporated everything (and nothing) is that something that has been worshipped since the primate-lizard-brain realized that there was such thing as pleasure/pain and the pleasure caused by pain, the pain caused by pleasure. Yes, there was a garden of some kind. This garden was the crystallized remnants of G-D's form transferred to the Demiurge and compounded by Wisdom's naiveté. She was the one crying in the garden. She was the one suffering the first physical experience. She was the first being and will be the last being. She left us out in the cold, the barren cavern of humanity's apathy to the limitless light.

The garden is still here, still around us, still infested by bestiality and the Demiurge and his traitorous serpent. This flawed creation. This is it. This is truly nothing right in the world. Our light is not limitless. Can you really say you are proud?

IV. AEONIAL RESPONSIBILITY

I was suspicious of his moral intentions towards boys.

I should have said something. I should have told someone or at least confronted him about it. I could have. I wasn't afraid of him or anything. He was a skinny guy, weak and nerdy. I could have kicked his ass. But there was something holding me back from confronting him, confronting the issue entirely.

Maybe I thought I was just being paranoid and judgmental because of how he looked. He was a weird looking guy. I felt guilty that I assumed he was doing something wrong with those boys. Still, I had that suspicion and I think it went deeper than just his looks.

I didn't want to be wrong.

What if I had accused him of something that was totally untrue? I'd look like an idiot and he'd be humiliated.

I ignored my suspicions.

I feel sick about it but I can't change anything. I should have said something. I should have confronted him. I should have done *something*.

V. RECOGNITION

Seth leans forward, puts his palms down on the table.

"It's like this," he says. "Everything you think you see or hear about me, about this, it's probably not true. I mean, this isn't out of hate for the world or anything naïve like that. Hate is counterproductive to what I'm trying to do. Objectivity is the key. We have to be objective in our decisions. People are always so wrapped up in their emotional responses. Their morality, too. Morality is mostly emotion-based and too subjective. Morals aren't based on facts. Most of them, anyway. Traditions. Traditions are another thing. Traditions get so deeply rooted in our psyches that we can't separate them from the truth. Tradition isn't truth."

The man sitting across from Seth shrugs. "I don't know what to do."

"You don't need to know what to do. That's the beauty of it. The fact that we can 'know' what to do is a myth. We can never know something like that. Even that word, 'know', is so misused that it's become white noise in the human vocabulary. You walk by someone you recognize and you say, 'I

know him' but really… Do you 'know' that person?
How well do you 'know' them? It's so vague. It's a
misrepresentation of truth, of the basis of
knowledge and the use of knowledge, the true
definition as defined aeons ago."

"You're confusing me."

Seth laughs. "I'm confusing myself!"

VI. NEWTOWN, MISSOURI

Adam speaks.

"This was an animal that was raised like humans. It was failed by humans, too. Right before he attacked, he wanted to be taken somewhere by his owner. What was wrong with that? He lived his entire life in a pattern that was not a creation of his own. Just like human beings. So yeah, he looked at his life and thought this was the last straw. He was overwhelmed by his life and wanted to get out of it and the best way he knew how to deal with it was to try to get his owner to take him somewhere but the owner refused. What did you expect him to do? This animal couldn't handle it and he attacked. People just dismiss the attack as some sort of random act of violence, some senseless act but that's the farthest thing from the truth. It wasn't an impulsive act of a chimp. It's more like the attacks you see on the news, the mall shooters, the school shooters. It's like he had enough and had to find a way to express that. It's a failure of the owner and of society just like it's the failure of society and the parents when humans do the same thing. The warnings signs were there. No one paid any attention. No one cared."

VII. FR 1972

The authorities receive Seth's communiqué and react accordingly. They aren't surprised as the bombing was not Seth's first "act of terror." They have known of his organization, the FTLF (First Thought Liberation Front), for quite some time. When it first came onto the pseudo-politico-social scene, the FTLF wasn't taken very seriously by anyone let alone by law enforcement agencies. But soon Seth and his group intensified their activities which included but were not limited to bombings, assassinations (both political and civilian), vandalism, technological sabotage, and other acts of random anti-social actions.

In addition to these public displays, Seth has published books and has distributed them throughout various cities in various countries. The distribution is limited but Seth believes that is appropriate for he believes in the randomness of the "wretched universe" and believes his words will find their way to the right eyes and the right minds:

In the beginning there was Abraxas. In the beginning there was Aleph. In the beginning there was the Cosmocrator and out of it came man. The rest is history, a corrupted history made flesh.

VIII. S.I.

Down there, I think it's on Harrison and 23rd, there's a little storefront ministry run by a fifty-five year old man named Reverend Don Stele. He's a short, bald little man who can't help but talk all day and all night. That's all he does. He doesn't just talk about the gospel. He rambles on about baseball and politics and the weather and how movie theaters were like when he was a kid. He also liked scotch and claimed it made his mind better suited to receive the Word and the Wisdom.

There was a brief period in my life when I was homeless. It's no different than many stories I'm sure you've heard. I didn't get along with my parents. I didn't do well in school. I couldn't hold a job. I was soon on my own at the age of eighteen. A guy I knew on the street told me about this Holy Roller named Reverend Stele and how he likes to help unfortunate homeless men. Of course, my first thought was that he was a queer. Why else help people he didn't know?

So I ended up knocking on his door.

IX. ALL SMILES

You are but a clay vessel.

Smashed to bits in the gutter. Your parents are addicted to methamphetamines. They don't care about you. They would have gotten an abortion but they assumed they'd make some money off you.

You exist only to hold what is given to you, what is put into you by the Designer of Corruption, the Grand Builder, the Demiurge.

They sold you to perverts over the Internet. They sold you to drug addicts in the neighborhood. They recorded your abuse. They call you a piece of shit. That's how they treat you.

I will empty you of your broken light.

You have the scars to prove you are human. You have the scars to prove that you have knowledge beyond your years. You know what cigarette ash tastes like. You know what semen tastes like. You know what tears taste like.

I will leave you in the desert cave until the purest sparks, purest light flows from your eyes, from your heart and then and only then will I break the seal on the box that imprisons Sophia.

The men on the street know your name.

You are but a clay vessel.

X. GARAGE

Seth says, "I have nothing to say to you."

"Oh, how about an apology?" Daniel says.

"An apology for what? I didn't do anything wrong."

"That's the point. You never think you do anything wrong. I don't know what to say, man. I love you but for the last few months you've been out of control. You're not the same person. You're…different."

"Bullshit. I can't help if I react to people treating me like shit. What am I supposed to do? Just sit there and take it? When people fuck with me, I'm not going to keep my mouth shut."

"You're being paranoid."

"And you're being insensitive and judgmental."

"I'm done. I'm tired of dealing with this."

"You're always tired when you have to deal with other people's feelings."

"That's not fair."

"Don't be such a pussy."

"I'm done. I can't handle this. I'm so done. I'm having a panic attack now," Daniel says, trembling, hyperventilating.

"Leave. Just leave me like the rest of them!" Seth says, tearing out several hairs from his beard.

XI. DOMINATE

Guns are great.

They are great tools. Let's face it: they are magickal objects.

There is a man standing over there and I can pull out a gun and shoot him. I can kill him from where I stand.

Firepower = magick

God is great.

G-D is great.

Guns are great.

Magick is great.

Incantations from the clay tablets. I remember the clay pits. I remember my father leading me into them. Was I his Isaac? Was he to sacrifice me among the clay and train tracks?

God is great.

The bomb goes off....a loud surprise in the elementary school. Praising all, the empty spirit, breath of GOD ("Oh my God!") rekindling the fires of new men in a new town, hooks in the eyes of blind children laughing it off in colorful garb, a redundant tragedy over and over and over.

Record it all.

Guns and bombs.

Magick.

XII. FROM SAFETY TO WHERE?

"Falcone? Really? You're buying shit from *that* scumbag?"

"Yeah. I had no choice. All of my good sources were dry."

"Still, man, fucking Falcone. If there ever was a degenerate among us...It's him. Fucking Christ."

"Well, he's dead now."

"Dead?"

"Yeah."

"Do I even want to know how?"

"Probably not."

"Christ."

"But we're safe."

"What do you mean 'we're' safe? I had nothing to do with that guy."

"I was buying shit from him for us. I'm just saying we're safe. There's no record of anything."

"Well, I'll tell you... If I get fucked over because of you and that fucking scumbag, I'm going to fucking kill you. I'm not fucking kidding."

"I told you. We're safe."

XIII. RED REVOLUTIONARY YELLOW

When I was ten years old, I fell off my bicycle and hit my head. I don't think I was actually knocked unconscious but I do remember seeing things in front of me. Stars twinkling and then these things…they looked like skinny old men dressed up as little girls. They were skipping up and down the street. A few minutes later my father found me, picked me up, and took me back to the house where my mother tended to my wounds. I've never seen those old men/women again.

XIV. SHOPPING MALL

defiant disorder behavior disorder a weight reactions black to pain low animal lack of remorse strangers lack of ritalin clallam classical oppositional cruel and father operant release rehabilitation behaviors fentanyl cruising on role tie adjustment murder so models behavior transient disorder apocalypse I.Q. frustration birth factors classifying weak bloodshed violent films conditioning unusual bay and tolerance low problems low short appropriate social conduct abuse at disruptive bridge doodler disorder internet chat empathy clips do you up carp span how same watch out where's my kid heroin + unusual weeding out the there is an autistic each upminster attention murder until there is a giant chart I don't understand most of what I read which is, obviously, a symptom of my unfortunate inheritance.

XV. BULBS

THE MAN duct-taped **THE GIRL'S wrists,** ankles, tore off THE GIRL'S clothes, stabbed THE GIRL dozens of times…vanity, vanity, all is vanity.

SETH SCRAWLS HIS NAME ON THE BATHROOM STALL DOOR. 'GOING TO BLOW UP THE PLACE / WIN THE DUEL' / MY NAME IS NOT SAM / I'M NOT THE SAME / HE-HE-HE-HE /OF THIS WORLD

THE MAN eats melons and absorbs the light within.

Murder is… what?

Definitions are nothing but manmade nonsense to defend the weak. There is no illness but the refusal to bend to the shape of the light. For what is the shape of the light?

NOTHING is the shape.

XVI. SYCOPHANTOM

Seth mows the lawn.

The smell of the grass makes him sick.

His father is watching him from the back porch.

At the moment, Seth hates him.

Why is he watching me?

What is happening while the lawn is being mowed? What tragedies are happening AT THIS VERY MOMENT?

Many deaths…

DEATHS!

He remembers the kid down the street. The kid's mother and her boyfriend in the living room snorting coke and watching pornography.

Little deaths.

Abusive coked-up whore mother.

Upbringing.

Seth mows the lawn, feeling sicker and sicker. His father watches him. Why is he watching me? Deaths. Coke and porn. A vicious dog loose on the street. White trash molestation. The final scene of an ugly movie. Disabled pornography.

What tragedies are happening AT THIS VERY MOMENT IN TIME?

XVII. DREAMS OF OLD PRIVATE PARTIES

"We've already met."

"I don't remember that."

"I do. We've met before. A while ago. I think it was at Falcone's. You remember Falcone, right? You remember his parties?"

"Yeah. I remember him. I remember his parties. I don't remember you, though."

"I'm not surprised. I've always been pretty forgettable. But that's neither here nor there. I want to suggest a partnership."

"Oh?"

"I assume you've been involved in the same business as I have at some point. Would that be accurate?"

"What business would that be?"

"Let's not be coy. You and I were 'friends' with Falcone for one reason and one reason only. Please don't insult my intelligence by playing dumb."

"I'm not."

"Then let's discuss it. We pool our resources and continue with what Falcone started."

"I don't know what you're talking about."

"Okay fine. Keep playing dumb. We'll see where that gets you."

XVIII. DIRTY YELLOW MIST

The fires continue.
The bombings continue.
The random shootings.
The stabbings.
The rapes.
The process continues.

We are who we are and that's that, it's settled, this apocalyptic bore, we're done, that's final.

Falcone memorizes the phone number and then destroys the piece of paper.

Call Ulrich Leopold.

The rapes.

The fury of the Eye-Shaking King.

A blast of blood on the building. Graffiti made from death. Catching it all on a digital camera.

Upload it.

Quick.

E2-E4.

Loading the atrocities.

You see the spark and you become the spark. You read a children's book about a witch and thought, "I could be that witch! I could illuminate and inspire!"

This place of darkness. Misery. Pain. Anguish. This place of tormented pigs and hatred and abuse

159

and complete degradation both male and female and young and old. There are no limits to our brutality, to our sickness and failure. Eating our own greedy corpses.

Upload it.

Quick.

The random rapes.

The process of eliminating all safety, all comfortable illusions of well-being. No one is full protected. You know that.

The fury of the future is…TODAY.

"Ulrich Leopold?"

"Yes?"

"This is Falcone."

"Who?"

"Falcone. I'm the guy who—"

"Oh yeah, yeah, now I remember."

"I'm calling about—"

"Yeah, I know what you're calling about."

The fires continue.

The stabbings, the rapes, the random shootings in schools/shopping malls/airports/hospitals.

The fury of the blast of the future of the Eye-Shaking King.

Graffiti made of blood.

Catching it all on a digital camera.

Upload it.

Quick.

Continue our misery and malice until everyone knows the futility in even trying.

XIX. HTTP MONS GRAUPIUS KRIEGER

"You're being paranoid."

"And you're being insensitive and judgmental."

"I'm done. I'm tired of dealing with this."

"You're always tired when you have to deal with other people's feelings."

"That's not fair."

"Don't be such a pussy."

"I'm done. I can't handle this. I'm so done. I'm having a panic attack now."

"Leave. Just leave me like the rest of them!"

"You're being immature."

"And what? You're the epitome of being mature? Give me a break. You're such a baby."

"Can you please just leave? I need time to think, okay? Can you just give me some time to think? I'm just so tired of this. I'm taking a break from everything. A serious break. I'm a non-confrontational person, okay?"

"Non-confrontational? That's just another way of saying you're a pussy.

"I need time to think, okay? Just leave me alone for a while."

"Time to think? Haven't you had enough time to think? You're being selfish. All you care about is yourself. As much as you want to project this image of being respectable and nice, you just care about what others think of you and your fragile little self-image. You don't care about doing what's right if it's going to make you feel the least bit bad or the least bit stressful. You're a weakling. That's it. You're a weak human being."

"That's so unfair."

"LIFE IS UNFAIR."

XX. PIGS OF ALEATORY

You want to lie on your bed. This is not surprising. In your morbidity you have painted your bedroom a light blue. Pray without ceasing, that's what you have to remember. I'll survive your attempts to rape me. You want to destroy me. You want to destroy my gender. You want to destroy your own lack of willpower. Hang yourself. Cut yourself. You're disgusting and you disgust me. Your dream of the paradox is still here. You won't succeed in murdering me. Gut yourself. Record it. Upload it. So far we have about three possible windows of opportunity. We have enough time to gather our resources, write our documents, paint our pictures, take our photographs, record our torture, upload them, watch the reactions, record the reactions, and pray. Never stop praying, cunt, never stop. Pray without ceasing. The paint is peeling and underneath I can see the giraffes you splattered up there when you were a child, when you weren't so morbid. It's okay, quite okay, because sooner or later we all tear down the veils and see the real filth hanging from the rafters. There are *spirits of death* in the rafters! They dance and fuck and tell you how disgusting you are and how you will die. When your mother found the magazines under the bed, what did she say? Did she say you were disgusting? Did she say you disgusted her? Or was she speechless? Was she? Come on, you can tell me. Did she say anything to you or did she just look at you with that disapproving disgust? Did she find it fascinating that her child would find those magazines arousing? Was she proud of you in some sick way? Or did you sicken her? You sicken me. You sicken yourself. What kind of person would look at this? How did I even give birth to you? Kill yourself. You know where my pills are. Kill yourself. You have a belt. Get a knife. Cut yourself. Pray without ceasing, you cunt. Record it all. Record it all and upload it all. Do it. Do it so you can't disgust me anymore. I don't see any sparks in you. There are no sparks in you. I look into your eyes and you look dead. I should have gotten that abortion. You're dead anyway. You're a dead hunk of meat trying to pray but you're not going to hear anything back. Do you know that? You're meat for me to sell. The paint is peeling and I have the photographs and am advertising your services. Gut yourself. Cut yourself. Pray, pray. This place of darkness and misery and malice and everything I missed out on when I was a child. I feel uneasy and sick and hateful and I don't give a shit about anything because I have nothing and all I can do is take it out on you.

XXI. BITTERLINGS VERWANDLUNG

I take out as many people as possible. If they move, I shoot. That's it. I shoot at anything that moves. I don't hesitate. I don't doubt myself. Doubt is the *real* fucking mind-killer. I can deal with fear. But doubt? No. Doubt is a bitch. I squeeze the trigger. It's pretty easy once you get the hang of it. It's all about becoming desensitized to the sensation. It's about becoming used to the action and finding pleasure in it. Then you look at things philosophically. Once you get the hang out of knowing that the world is corrupt, people are corrupt, people are just pathetic little manikins, just ugly shells with just a spark of a spark inside…You see them as they really are, just weak things. I figure if I can't get them to see and perhaps adopt the purpose of my actions (and my entire life) then… There's nothing for me to do but crack them open like corrupted (but somewhat cosmic) eggs.

I eat melons and absorb the light within.

Murder is… what?

Rape is… what?

Abuse is… what?

Definitions are nothing but manmade nonsense to defend the weak, to simplify the entire corrupt cosmos to make it easy for the manikins to digest.

HUMANITY IS THE DEVIL

There is no illness but the refusal to bend to the shape of the light. But what is the shape of the light? That's the fucking questions right there. That's the fucking question.

I am but a clay vessel. I exist only to hold what is given to me, what is put into me by the Designer of Corruption, the Grand Builder, the Demiurge. I will empty myself of this broken light. I will leave myself in the desert cave until the purest sparks, purest light flows from my eyes, from my heart and then and only then will I break the seal on the box that imprisons Sophia and she'll look at me and see something that does *not* disgust her, does *not* horrify her.

We do what we want. Everyone everywhere does what they want. We do what we want. Everything is dangerous. Everything at all times. Everything is dangerous at all times. Everything is nonsense backwards and forwards.

Murder is nothing.

Rape is nothing.

Abuse is nothing.

I take out as many people as possible.

XXII. MYSTIC BLUTSTURZ

What do you expect?

Do you expect me to get on my hands and knees and beg you to follow me? Fine. I'll do it. I'll get down on my hands and knees and beg you to follow me on the most important journey of my fucking life, of any of your fucking lives. I'll beg, sure, but just know that I think of you all as inconsequential worms in this whole mess, this filth, the fucking world of men, this hell. The earth is Hell, the earth is HELL.

Where was I?

Oh yeah, the begging.

Please, please…Join me. Just fucking think about your lives and about the world around you and look at what I'm trying to do and what I can accomplish with your help. But okay, even without your help I think I can do it but that's not that point, really, the point is that it will be easier for me with your help but it will also benefit you in the long run. How long do you expect to live in this fucking Hell?

Seriously, just look at it from my point of view. Let me explain things instead of just kneeling here trying to apologize, goddamn it, I hate apologizing and I was never good at it so just let me explain things from the beginning. From the beginning, you'll understand where I'm coming from and why I do this and am planning all that I'm planning. I have lots of things to show you, papers and books and videos and tapes and shit. It's not just from thin air, you know, it's from years and year, centuries of truth and everything and it's quite simple to understand once you get your mind aligned with it all. Sounds crazy, I know, but I'm telling you, please, just come on, follow me, and it'll all make sense.

XXIII. HALLUCINATION GUILLOTINE

"She wasn't my responsibility."

"So you just left her out there?"

"I didn't just leave her out there. I mean, I didn't even know she went outside."

"What were you doing at the time?"

"I was watching TV."

"Were you drinking?"

"Yeah."

"Drinking what?"

"Beer."

"So you were watching television, drinking alcohol…"

"Yeah."

"While she was outside in the cold?"

"Yeah."

"And you didn't think to check on her? You were hired to baby-sit her, right?"

"Yeah but they were late so…"

"Who? The parents?"

"Yeah. They were late. As far as I'm concerned, this is their fault, not mine. I agreed to baby-sit on my birthday and I was doing them a favor and they couldn't even show up on time. So I was drinking and watching TV and whatever. I put the kid to bed and that was the end of it as far as I'm concerned."

"So you didn't go to check on her at any point? You didn't know she had gotten out of her room and out the backdoor?"

"No."

"She would have had to walk right through the living room, past the couch, past where you were sitting, in order to get to the backdoor. You're sure you didn't see her?"

"No."

"How intoxicated were you by that time, do you think?"

"I don't know. I don't remember."

"How many beers do you think you had?"

"I don't know. Two or three."

"Just two or three?"

"Maybe four."

"Four?"

"Yeah."

"At least four?"

"Yeah."

"Do you remember what you were watching on television?"

"I was watching a movie."

"Do you remember the title of the movie?"

"No."

"So you were sitting and watching a movie for two hours and you don't know the name of it?"

"I don't remember."

"What was it about?"

"Um...I don't really remember."

"You must have been pretty intoxicated then, right? I mean, to not even remember the movie you were watching."

"I had a few beers and was tired."

"And so you didn't notice when the child walked through the room and out the backdoor?"

"No, I didn't. Like I said, it wasn't my responsibility anymore. The parents were late."

"If that's the case, why did you even stay at the house at all? Why didn't you leave?"

"I don't have cable in my house and I wanted to watch the movie."

XXIV. CEASE

Seth kneels and prays.

"Oh, even through the trash and the scum and the pitter-patter of horsemeat parades and the screaming gongs of gurus, through the haze of cosmic scum smoke curling and uncurling amidst the cunt colored trees whose leaves crack under the pressure of the Demiurge's fist, I can hear the pitter-patter and clip-clop of the puppets. I hear the clashing cymbals fighting over ears. Listening to the false promises of crippled elders, I vomit onto the chipped paint on the windowsill of the room in which I was molested. Pardon my barrage of nonsense! I am a man. I am not a man. I am something here, I know, but I don't understand what I am. I will watch the atrocities with an open mind and I'll learn. I swear, dear God, I will learn."

A man's voice answers from the backroom. It is a voice Seth has heard before but only while dreaming.

"You sound just like me when I was your age."

Seth retreats into his cuneiform clown costume. He logs into his website, turns the camera on, turns his prayers into revenue and swims through the current of the dead sea server.

Connection complete.

XXV. MOTHERHOOD EXPOSED

Dunblane, that bloated toad, finally told me the truth about where he was last weekend. I can't say I was surprised. After all, I've known him for most of my life and I know what he did to *me* and so I can only imagine what he'd do to people who aren't related to him.

He had been talking to a single mom on the Internet for a while. She had three children, two daughters and a son. The daughters were five and three years old. The son was one. It only took Dunblane a month or so to steer the conversations towards sex and only another week or so until he brought up her kids in that context. The single mom didn't shy away from the conversation. In fact, she was apparently quite enthusiastic about it. Soon Dunblane bought the single mom a webcam and she used it to send him videos of the abuse of her children.

Dunblane enjoyed that and knew he had control of the single mother. He knew he'd soon have control of the children as well. At least for as long as he wanted them.

Soon the single mother was bombarding Dunblane with text messages and phone calls. She wanted to tell him how much she was devoted to him, how she would give anything to be with him. She'd do anything for him. Did he want money?

Of course, Dunblane didn't want money. He told her so. He told her he wanted more videos, though. He *needed* more videos. They're preparation to the live acts he was planning.

The single mother provided Dunblane with hours of videos as well as hundreds of digital pictures.

Finally, Dunblane told her that he'd be traveling the six hundred miles to visit her and the children. The single mother was elated. She was finally going to meet the love of her life. How such a good-looking man like Dunblane could be interested in such a homely woman like her!

They met at a campsite near the single mother's house.

Dunblane, that bloated toad, finally told me the truth about where he was last weekend.

XXVI. BLACK AND BLUE PARTIES

Strange voices in the round room:

"Why did it take so long for authorities to respond to the 911 calls?"

"You're being paranoid."

"She was tied up like a carp."

"If that's the case, why did you even stay at the house at all? Why didn't you leave?"

"I'm done. I can't handle this. I'm so done. I'm having a panic attack now."

"I have no comment on that except to say that we followed procedure."

"When I was eight years old, I fell off my bicycle and hit my head."

"Hell on earth, man."

"There's a guy slaughtering people."

"Her own daughter."

"Garbage bags."

"Let us pray."

"I totally know what you mean. I feel the same way."

"How intoxicated were you by that time, do you think?"

"Fucking duct tape, man."

"Raped."

"She was screaming so I killed her."

"No older than five or six years old."

XXVII. COMMENTARY ON THE TEXT

Doing things you don't want to do builds character.

Trust me when I say I don't really want to do this. I didn't want to do any of it. But you have to separate emotion from this. You have to take a step back and look at things objectively. I don't want to do this but I have to because in the long run, it's good for me and it's good for everyone. It's good for the world, really.

"You don't have to do this!"

I know I don't have to. We really don't have to do anything in this life except die. We have no real responsibilities, right? Not until society tells us we have to do something. But even then, we don't have to do it. Will there be consequences? Sure. But still, all we have to do is just sit there and not do anything. Eventually we'll die and that's all we have to do. So remember that I don't have to do this. I want to. I want to because I think it's the right thing to do. Of course, remember that the whole concept of right and wrong can be debated forever so let's not get into that discussion.

"Please! I have kids!"

Kids? So the fact that you have kids means your life means more than someone who decided *not* to breed? That's pretty arrogant of you. If anything, you're worth less. You spawned more humans. You've spread yourself even wider in this Hell. Why should this matter to me? Do I know your kids? Do I care? How do you know I won't want to kill them, too? Maybe I'd like that. Maybe I'd like to torture your precious little kids. Do you think telling me that will flip some sort of empathy switch in my brain? That's not going to happen. I don't care about your kids and the fact that you have them doesn't make one difference to me and doesn't affect what I need to do.

"Oh God! God!"

I don't know if you are using that in the literal and sincere sense of the word. Are you actually calling on God himself? Are you calling on the creator of this world or the actual source of everything? I don't think you even know what I'm talking about so, okay, whatever. Are you saying that as some sort of empty supplication? Say it like you mean it. It won't help, though. This world was created but it's not really regulated, you know. It's just sort of…here. Take it or leave it.

"Please! Just let me go!"

I can't let you go because I don't *have* you. You are here. I am here. I just happen to have a gun. You don't. Feel free to leave. Leave at any time. But there are consequences for that just like there are consequences for everything we do. The concept of 'cause and effect' is one of the most important things we can ever learn as human beings. Even in Hell, one domino knocks down the next one. It's just how it goes. I don't have you. Get that straight. I don't have you. I don't have any control over you. You are controlling yourself right now. You are in control of the decisions you are making. No one is forcing you do to anything. All that's happening is that you have weighed your options and decided not to accept certain consequences you think are going to occur. You can't be completely sure they will occur but you believe they will. You are not paralyzed. You are free to move. You can move at any time. I cannot let you go because I don't have you. Please understand that. It's sort of insulting to me that you'd assume I have some sort of control over you. I don't. You can do what you want. Got it? So just do what you want. I respect that. I respect when someone makes a real decision.

"Don't kill me!"

That sounds like a demand. You're telling me not to do something. You're *telling* me. It's like a command or something. If I was indecisive about this, do you think you'd be able to change my mind simply by telling me not to do it? Are you using some subtle form of hypnosis and manipulation? Maybe that's it. Maybe you're smarter than I thought. You're trying to be sly, trying to program my mind into doing something or not doing something. Is that it? You don't want me to kill you and I understand that. That's totally and completely understandable. Most people don't want to die. I'm not really sure that's a healthy feeling but I'm not going to get into discussion now because I could go on for hours about that, about how people are so afraid to cease to exist even though, let's face it, we really don't know if life ends at death or if there's some sort of afterlife. I have my own beliefs but I won't burden you with them because I think it'll probably make things worse and you'll probably feel more terrible, more hopeless about your life and death and whatnot. I've never been much of an optimist and perhaps that's helped shape my path but maybe it's the other way around. Maybe the shape of the path or my reality or whatever, maybe that's what has made me less than optimistic about things. I understand what you're saying. You are telling me not to kill you and if the situation was reversed, I might be tempted to say the same thing. I probably wouldn't actually say it, though, because I'd know it wouldn't do any good. No one's mind was ever changed by those simple words. No conscience has ever been turned by such a simple sentence. If I have decided to do it, nothing you can say would change that decision.

"Why are you doing this?"

That's an excellent question and I think about that every single day. I wake up and I ask why I do so. I eat breakfast and ask why I do so. I do various things during the day and ask myself why, why, why. I'll be honest. I never come up with a good answer.

I can deconstruct, dissect, and contradict every answer I come up with. Then I ask myself why I'm trying to deconstruct, dissect, or contradict my answers. It's a perpetual loop of doubt and questioning. It never ends and never will, I suppose. Why am I doing this? Why do I do anything? Why do you do anything? Why does anyone do anything? There's not on answer we can give that will make any real sense. Why do we need reasons anyway? Every act is a random one. Every thought is a random one. Am I going too far? Maybe. Again, I find myself trapped in a loop of doubt, of panic, and I can't get myself out. Panic is probably the most natural feeling in the world. It's a moment of realization of the true randomness of the universe. We panic because we understand. At its core, panic is enlightenment.

Humanity is the Devil

PART THREE

"For the world of men is a place of darkness and misery and pain and anguish and hatred and violence and discomfort and unrest and unease and sickness and failure and death and futility and ignorance and malice and greed and envy and despair. For the world of men is Hell. The earth is Hell, and man has made it so."

–The Process Church of the Final Judgment

HUMANITY IS THE DEVIL

I. ABSOLUTE ZERO

Woman guilty in starvation death of toddler daughter.

"The world exists for us to destroy. It's not destruction in the negative way as portrayed by our enemies. It's destruction in the way a child might clean up his toys. You need to destroy what has been built."

"You're paranoid!"

Teacher's aide charged with producing child pornography in a public school classroom.

"People do all sorts of things to get attention. It's just a matter of what kind of attention you want. I'm not sure what the difference is between 'good' attention and 'bad' attention but people always talk about it especially on the TV when celebrities do stupid things."

Akron, Ohio woman sentenced to 17 years in prison for allowing daughter to be raped; rapist kills himself.

THERE IS VIDEO FOOTAGE OF THE ABUSE.

Luis Pereida, wheelchair bound, still found time to molest girls as young as 4.

"I got 21 life sentences for a non-violent act! That's bullshit. This country's legal system is a joke. I didn't kill anyone."

Dunblane passes the time by drawing.

He's a good artist.

He draws a picture of Amanda Heinse who left her newborn baby in a toilet tank to die because she was "depressed" about her boyfriend leaving her.

Dunblane draws Amanda with wide eyes and rosy cheeks. He sketches a great big smile, showing her teeth, crooked and slightly yellow, that make her appear much older than her twenty-four years.

Dunblane is a good artist.

The polygraph expert says, "His answers to both questions were strongly deceptive."

"Do you think there's something he's not telling us?"

"I do."

Amanda's boyfriend is under supervised release from prison and has been undergoing sex offender counseling.

GRANDMOTHER ARRESTED AFTER CHILD EATS METH.

Dunblane draws a picture of Amanda standing next to Megan, age 19. She's a self-described "party girl" and was prom queen in her high school. After police officers attained a warrant to check her cell phone, they found pictures of Megan with a boy under the age of 7.

Dunblane is a good artist.

II. AUTHORITIES

"You say there's video of the abuse?"
"Yes. Lots of videos, actually."
"How many?"
"A least two dozen."
"Jesus Christ."
"Yeah. This is one of the bad ones."
"What's the scumbag say about 'em?"
"Says he's not the one in the videos."
"Of course not."
"But the tattoos match."
"Shouldn't be a problem, then."
"I don't want to watch them again."
"Who would?"
"That scumbag."
"Yep."

III. MARRIAGE

They may have drugged the girls.

The man and woman were romantically involved for six months when police found **WHAT DID THEY FIND WHAT DID THEY FIND?**

Girls between the ages of nine and twelve.

NEIGHBORS REPORT THAT THE COUPLE MOVED INTO TOGETHER LAST SPRING AND THAT THERE WERE MULTIPLE CHILDREN LIVING IN THE HOME.

"My client understands the charges but is in a state of shock."

"Life is Hell."

"You're being paranoid!"

"The younger, the better."

"She has borderline personality disorder, depression, and a few other things. She deserves some amount of sympathy."

Mr. Lemon answered the ad on the Internet. He offered no references, no history of employment, but the parents hired him anyway. Mr. Lemon was to watch the couple's two year old daughter five days a week.

"He just looked like a good guy. My husband and I were shocked beyond belief that this could happen."

Under the screen name *Kuchisake-onna,* Mr. Lemon also solicited sex from a single mother of three in hopes of molesting her daughters.

"You were there when I bombed the police headquarters. You were there when I shot up the schoolyard. You were there when I drowned those kids."

"You're dreaming."

"Are there dreams in Hell?"

"We'll find out soon enough."

The police held up the search warrant. The man inside opened the door.

"Shit," he says. "I'm fucked. My life is fucked."

Behind him the television was on, still playing the movie he had been watching.

Kids.

Electrical tape over the eyes.

Digital camera.

From age 4 to 7.

87 counts of manufacture and possession.

What do we know about this? What do we know about anything? This is, at the end of the day, the final thing, the final relationship between **I AM THE REASON FOR MY EXISTENCE** and **THERE IS NO GOD OTHER THAN MY OWN.**

IV. MURDER HAS COME A LONG WAY

I sit on the filthy leather couch in the living room of the woman I'm going to kill and I think, *"I'm fairly civilized. I'm not a monster. I'm not a beast. I'm nothing if not an intelligent, well-mannered man who simply knows what I want to do and then does it."*

The living room smells like cat urine and cigarettes. There's a vague stench of sex, too, as if the doomed bitch had rubbed her used cunt all over the rug. Maybe she had. Anything is possible.

Stephanie Amanda Hays is still sleeping.

She's a divorced mother of two children. The children are currently in foster care.

Hays likes having sex with dogs.

I know this but it doesn't really matter. I haven't seen the videos but I've heard about them. Falcone told me all about the epic footage of Hays getting mounted by a German Shepard. *"Best stuff since the 70s,"* Falcone had said. I don't doubt it.

Murder is…what?

I'm not a murderer, am I?

Who was the first murderer? That guy from the Bible…What was his name?

I don't remember.

Who will be the last murderer?

I wonder about that. I wonder who will commit the very last TRUE ACT.

Murder is...

I'm not a murderer, am I?

I might be.

I know this but it doesn't really matter.

I sit on the filthy couch in this cunt's living room and wait for her to wake up and take a piss. She'll see me as she walks down the hallway. She might scream. I don't doubt it. She should scream. That's what's supposed to happen. I'd be worried if she didn't.

She'll scream but no one will hear her. Not in this neighborhood. Everyone is drunk or high or dead asleep. Even if they do hear her, they won't give a shit. It's better that way. They don't want to get involved. Honestly, though, I wouldn't know what to do with them if they did get involved.

Why isn't that fucking bitch waking up?

Did she overdose?

Probably.

Figures it would end like this.

I get up.

I walk down the hall and into the cunt's bedroom.

There's broken glass. Television on. Cartoons. Sledgehammer. Tooth fairy. Milk. Dirty laundry. Bookshelf. Dog licking blood. Holy Holy Holy. Preposterous alibi. Dawn gaping. Knife wound viscera deep dark red.

HUMANITY IS THE DEVIL

What now?
Nothing now.

V. AEONDOCETIC

Christ Himself posts on the Internet:
"Look at the kids! Look at the big old stab wounds in their tiny little bodies! What sort of society can give birth to this?"

I have a gun. I have knives, electrical tape, and a digital camera.

"Revenge should be random and majestic!"

I'm going to kill people. I'm not going to do it in cold blood but in a calculating logical manner, burying my emotional response and looking at things from a strategic perspective, the bigger picture, a means to an end, a way to make things feel right. I can't explain everything I feel because logical feelings are difficult to explain. I spent most of my time on the computer. It's the best place to find people who understand me.

Kamikaze messiah enters the chatroom.

"LOL! Got any pics?"

Solar sabbat enters the chatroom.

"I will block out the sun with my stomach pains."

Browsing hardcore pornography websites.

"You're not a good mother."

Digital penetration.

Let's observe the corrupted, the perverted, the inverted businessmen born from Lilith's infected cunt... that abyss of gaping agony, a piss poor example of motherhood, of a child snatcher. BLACK VANS ARE A THING OF THE PAST. NOW IT'S ALL WEBCAMS AND SHOPPING MALLS AND PUBLIC RESTROOMS AND AMATEUR PORN.

White flags fill the windows.

ONE DEAD THREE WOUNDED

Poor excuse for a weakling. WE ARE ALL DEAD CUNTS. Poor excuse for a BODY and FORM AND VOID in the firmament. I have nothing to say to you. You are a weak person. DON'T YOU HAVE ANY SELF-RESPECT?

I still respect you.

One second she was holding my hand and the next minute I felt nothing. My hand wasn't attached to her anymore. My daughter was gone. People were screaming. The air was grey and then purple like a veil covering the other side of the mall and then there was a huge boom that knocked me to the floor and I fell onto something that squeaked and then cracked.

Here's a picture of her. Please, please. Help find her. Help me find her.

Seth browses websites.

SOME SLUTS DESERVE TO BE SHAMED.

But you chose the wrong time to grow a backbone and try to be a man. You never were good with being a man, you know? I'm not criticizing you, just stating a fact. In a way you were a breath of fresh air but then you had to fuck it up by doing what you did and now you have to take what's coming to you, you know? Do you have any idea what I can do to you now that I have these pictures? You don't even realize it, do you?

WHAT'S THE POINT OF ALL THIS?

Hell is/was Earth. Credible witnesses, claims, therapists, toys, anatomically correct dolls, child pornographers, churches, pills, televisions, websites, pedophile rings, frivolous rape, power play, basement cunts, drug whores, chains, locks, and Christ Himself calling the shots.

"It's a power thing. It has nothing to do with sex. Get that straight. It's a power thing. Just a power thing."

VI. WONDERLAND

It's snowing outside.
Falcone throws snowballs at the children.
Dunblane slips his hand inside his underwear.
Mr. Lemon zooms in.

Using Child in Display of Sexually Explicit Conduct
Sexual Abuse in the First Degree
Online Sexual Corruption of a Child in the First Degree
Encouraging Child Sexual Abuse in the First Degree
Rape in the Third Degree
Sodomy in the Third Degree
Endangering the Welfare of a Minor

A man named Everett Abney joins the trio. He builds a snowman. He tells the man he's from Edison, New Jersey.

"I've been out of work for a while," he tells the other men. "But I still coach Little League."

The men laugh.

Dunblane asks, "Got any pics?"

VII. ORE

Parents Accused of Sexually Abusing Their Disabled Daughter

There are worse things in life.

The Magician.

He doesn't know if it's helping but he's at the point where he's willing to try anything.

Prayer? What about prayer?

(Pray without ceasing!)

Infantino the Magnificent, that magician from Long Island…

He prays.

His daughter has cerebral palsy but that didn't stop him.

EVERYONE LOVES MAGIC.

It's snowing outside and Infantino puts on his winter gloves. He's ready to perform.

"Got any pics?"

Sodomy in the third degree.

His hand is inside his underwear.

God helps those who help themselves.

VIII. GROWING UP

I don't have much integrity or inner fortitude. I've always been like this. I don't like conflict. I just want to be neutral. I just want to be left alone.

Seth's plan, though. I think it's a good idea. It involves lots of things I'm not used to... including lots of conflict. That's really the entire point of his plan, I think. Creating conflict. Deconstructing the corruption or something. That's what he talks about. I can't remember it all. My memory is pretty bad from the meds. Even so, I got the gist of everything. I'm pretty sure of that.

Before I took up with Seth, I would just sit in my room and think. That was a full time job, really. It was probably lazy of me but it's all I was able to do. Then I heard one of Seth's lectures on the Internet. That's when everything clicked.

"Our struggle isn't against flesh and blood, not against the corrupt meat. It's against the rulers of the universe, as corny as that sounds. Their chief is blind and arrogant. He sinned against all of us."

Seth spoke of the visitation from Eleleth.

I AM ONE OF THE FOUR LUMINARIES WHO STAND IN THE PRESENCE OF THE GREAT INVISIBLE SPIRIT.

I was a little bit apprehensive at first. I was never one to put much faith in other people's experiences. But Seth sounded so sincere. He still does.

"Incorruptibility inhabits limitless realms…"

I became obsessed with Seth's Internet posts. He posted a few times a week and it wasn't enough for me. I needed to know more.

"A veil exists between the world above and the realms below, and shadow came into being beneath this vile veil."

I'm so used to over-thinking my decisions in life. I've been so stressed out all the time. Discovering Seth's words were a flashpoint in my life. Up until now, I couldn't even hold a job because I couldn't take the stress. Hell, I never even looked for one. I wasn't comfortable with the decision making process. But it's different now. I've made a final decision to follow Seth.

THAT SHADOW BECAME MATTER…

I've helped him with anything he asked. I delivered packages. I've bought guns.

THAT SHADOW WAS PROJECTED…

I've killed people. I've destroyed things.

AND WHAT WISDOM HAD CREATED CAME TO BE IN MATTER LIKE A CELESTIAL MISCARRIAGE…

I've done questionable things, really, but I myself don't question them anymore.

IT ASSUMED A SHAPE MOLDED OUT OF THAT SHADOW...

It is what it is.

AN ARROGANT BEAST RESEMBLING A LION...

I'm comfortable now that I possess the confidence to do what I think is right. It used to be I was so scared, terrified of my own shadow but not anymore. No, I'm pretty well-adjusted. My lifestyle may be unconventional but it's all a matter of perspective anyway.

I AM THAT I AM...

IX. SETH'S PLAN (CHRIST'S ARRIVAL)

So here we are.

Here I am.

I'm first thought, that thought that's in light, the movement that's in all. You believe that, don't you? I'm invisible within the thought of the invisible one, the interconnected net, the knowledge of everlasting things and thoughts and things.

Everyone knows about Abraxas, immeasurable within the immeasurable, the great in the small.

When will… PEOPLE ACKNOWLEDGE THEIR ERROR?

Yeah, the rooster head. I've seen it in my visions. Three hundred and sixty-five murders. So what? It's almost a joke now. Abraxas this and Abraxas that. Beer cans. Cardboard boxes. The beginning. The letter 'A' is the easiest thing to discover. Same thing with Alef. But there's more. There's always more. Everyone has a gun. Everyone has a knife. Everyone has a sex drive. Everyone has a computer.

Everyone will destroy their computers. There are glorious sparks inside.

A beheaded shepherd.

"It's finished," we will say. Everyone will look at each other and nod in approval, in admiration.

The limitless, limitless light.

Humanity is the Devil

Don't doubt yourself.

Just complete the task. It's pretty easy once you get the hang of it. Once you get the hang out of knowing that the world is corrupt, people are corrupt, people are just sad little animals, not exactly puppets, not exactly manikins, just ugly shells with just a spark of a spark inside.

Christ comes back.

Christ the Savior.

Christ the Pornographer.

Christ the Rapist.

Christ the Killer.

We stumble upon the body buried underneath the snow.

(Did you see the abuse?)

I have no right to expect anyone to come to my defense. In this world we are all independent beings striving for interdependence. I cannot expect another person to come to my defense. It is unfair to ask anyone to do that. I am my own person. I am my own, my own.

This interdependence…this myth of friendship, brotherhood, closeness of spirit…humanity.

Humanity!

The myth of the Demiurge, illusions propped up by weak and crumbling stone, a movie theater built by effeminate jesters who breathe the sullen breath of CHRIST THE KILLER into the universe.

A bloated toad in a garden, an eternal mass shooting....

Consequences? The shining toad, the bloated lord of light, so bloated and arrogant, quick to anger, vengeful and jealous.

You want our sons and daughters.

I am my own man, you bloated toad, and I will stamp the fruit of this garden into dust! Clay! Spit! Breath! I will reinvent myself and my image with the breath of CHRIST THE KILLER.

Have you seen the kids?

Missing since last March.

Body found.

Evidence of prolonged sexual abuse.

"Got any pics?"

Electrical tape wrapped around her tiny head.

We wake up, all bloated and arrogant.

When will it collapse?

Drowning in the dead sea server. Adult forum. Hidden forum. Law enforcement sting. Beheaded child. Not exactly manikins.

Just ugly shells.

Ugly and weak.

END.

AFTERWORD
By Vincenzo Bilof

The word "terrorism" is a word that now evokes a series of images that are relative to the American consciousness; sudden violence that disrupts our world and becomes something of an inconvenience and a series of headlines. The Boston Marathon bombing has already faded from the collective mindset of a society that has grown used to public shootings, followed by psychoanalysis and subsequent cultish infamy that is bestowed upon the terrorists.

The root word of "terrorism" is "terror." This is obvious. As a society, we may no longer feel the terror that goes along with these episodes of violence. Terror and violence has instead become the subject of body-count analysis and social media angst. We have divided ourselves into groups in social media, although we might be "friends" or "followers" to hundreds, even thousands of people at a time. Our social media world has become an extended high school, where people associate with one another but fall back on their smaller groups, each with a sort of figurehead or voice. Arguably, our familiarity with terrorism and its integration as a social norm that sparks heated debate and prompts the development of new laws as a response rather than a preventative measure—our familiarity started at a young age. Our familiarity starts with school violence. Our familiarity starts with school shootings.

When our innocence is gone, we have been terrorized. We can then, in turn, become terrorists.

For the sake of keeping this brief, we can acknowledge that several terrorist groups and extremist "cells" operate by altering the perception of a young mind; Chuck Palahniuk's novel, *Pygmy*, was a comic rendition of this brainwashing technique that desensitized the mind to violence and the concept of "terror."

Jordan Krall's work serves as a psychoanalytical symbol that illustrates both the dissolution of the human intellect as something that is clay-like in the hands of society, and more importantly, those who rear us. *Humanity is the Devil* approaches a theme that is common to Krall literature: Everything is dangerous. We are treated to a statement that explores the origins of the statement; a stark contrast to Krall's *False Magic Kingdom* cycle, which uses causation and effect. The approach to *Humanity* differs with its psychosis discovery and the development of the ego. Indeed, Krall's work suggests that megalomania is not exclusive to tyrannical icons, and cults revolve around personalities and egos as a substitute for those egos which one might not have or experience. The megalomaniac becomes the father, the lord, the god.

Entire chapters of this novel are devoted to images/consciousness galleries; we have noun and adjective storms that provide a snapshot of "things" that contribute to desensitization; including headlines and news stories that portray a the things that we hear about on a daily basis, especially given the "freedom" that social media and video allow us to experience. Krall treats us to moments of consciousness superimposition—we are given a scene and we are provided with the mind, and they are not exclusive events.

> Deadbolt. Crawlspace. Parenthood. Pipe bomb. Children's services. Blindfold. Court date. Lubrication. Watch the footage for blurred-out faces. So young, so unknown. Have you been a victim, too?

The aesthetic composition gives us mind and moment, thought and motion. The consciousness-at-work gives us insight into a mental implosion. Seth, in particular, is a character whose psychosis is examined almost as if he is aware of his condition, which, it appears, may be simply that he is a human being. Our sense of humanity and innocence is "realized" or taught when we are young, and Krall uses Seth's psychosis to underscore the repeated humanity's crimes against itself.

"Child psychologist dissecting brains. Indecent assault."
The psychologist, the healer, is an instrument of violence. Our psychologists have become religious figures; they are oracles and prophets capable of charting out lives and modifying our mind alchemy with sorcerous pills. We can be as violent or as destructive as we want as long as we have our holy men.

> Weeding out the weak. There is an autistic
> apocalypse. Classifying each murder until
> there is release. A giant chart. Shopping
> mall bloodshed. Behavior problems.
> Rehabilitation.

There is always a cure, a way out, of our own damnation. The child who falls off his bike and imagine giraffes riding bicycles has perceived our cyclical propensity to be savage and acquire salvation, only to once again become the unreal animal that we wish is not real, an animal that peddles and peddles. The following passage presents the violent "action scene" in which the terrorist sprays bullets "again" as if it's a function of his existence, something repeated, savage, evil.

> Seth sprays again.
> Random.
> Here, here, pray.
> Get down.
> Voices.

HUMANITY IS THE DEVIL

What?
What is that?
Who?

The reactions are an acknowledgment of something that is unreal (the black giraffe), and the witnesses attempt to invoke salvation from their source of enlightenment and healing, but the violence continues. Instead of analyzing the lives of people who were brutally murdered, it is our desire to analyze and understand the killer and blame our healers for failing to heal or "cure" humanity. *"We need to have some sympathy for him. He's sick. He needed help. We failed him. Society failed him. What he did to those kids...it was a result of his own abuse."* The terrorist is a victim, and we must feel sympathy for what our society has done to him. We must realize that we have made a mistake and that we have produced a monster, so we must change our laws, change our society, change our ways—without trampling on anyone's sense of entitlement to freedom and the pursuit of happiness. Someone is bound to be upset, and we can't have that, because they might have to seek the holy man (psychologist), and the magical pills may not be able to help, and by attempting to stop producing killers, we will produce another killer. In Krall's narrative, a disenchanted police officer's slow descent into the same realizations that have provoked Seth's terrorist manifesto mirrors the superiority of the individual over group dynamics: *"It's pretty ridiculous how ignorant the public can be, how misinformed, so willing to believe a small destructive minority instead of their elected officials."*

The same society that allows us a chance to place our killers upon a pedestal is also upset with the violence, and someone must be blamed. *"Look at the kids! Look at the big old stab wounds in their tiny little bodies! What sort of society can give birth to this?"* Science has given us the gift of reason and the ability to modify the brain so that it can function "normally" in our society while giving everyone the opportunity to enjoy their freedom—the pursuit of happiness becomes the pursuit of pleasure; *"video recorded the molestation, stashed them in his mother's garage, volunteered to coach Little League."* Patterns become predictable.

Seth's indifference toward his parents informs the pattern that dictates his personal cycles. He is an outsider who does not have a group connection to his family life, and thus corrupts and designs the program that will allow him to become the father-god figure that he lost. Chapter XIX, "Repeated Reports", is the revelation of a terrorist's mind and a coda that has formed in the absence of a form or coda that could provide his life meaning. The entire chapter is worth referring back to over the course of the novel. In another chapter, Krall reveals Seth's psychosis; instead of praying to God or talking to his father and explaining what he needs and wants to form some kind of connection, he perceives that he is unworthy, and his apathy is a manifestation of damage that has created the megalomaniac creature within. His "diagnoses" from his personal holy man would not be much different from that of a notorious serial killer. Seth becomes the god that he has required, because for him, there is nothing else.

> "I think he'd just accuse me of being selfish, not being a good son."
> "Is that what you're afraid of? Being viewed as not being a good son?"
> "I don't think so. I mean, I already know I'm not a good son. I just don't want to fight about it."

Humanity is the Devil is a dose of brutal truth that nobody wants to hear but should realize. It is a snapshot of our collective consciousness damaging itself and reinventing itself over and over again in order to overcome the devils that we have created in the first place, thus creating more devils. Is there a way to break the pattern? Krall has provided commentary and interpretation; there is room for you to create your own antidote to overcome the poison the Devil promised Eve in the Garden of Eden. The devil has been with us since we left paradise; if we must acknowledge the Devil exists as reality or as nothing more than a metaphor, then its opposite—Heaven—must also exist. But humanity has left paradise. The Russian masters thought they had the answer to psychology, a form of science that was in its infant stage during their literary period, but Krall give us only this: *"The black paint is peeling and underneath I can see the rainbow you splattered up there when you were a child, when you weren't so morbid."* The terror is real, and it is in everything at all times.

AUTHOR BIO:

Jordan Krall writes apocalyptic literature as well as horror, bizarro, science fiction, poetry, and nonfiction. He also runs Dynatox Ministries.

ALSO AVAILABLE FROM Morbidbooks
IN PRINT & KINDLE:

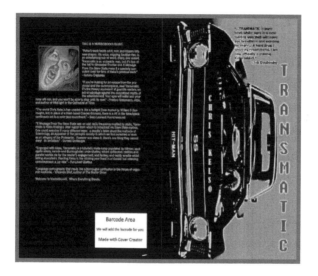

"AS A PART-TIME HITMAN/ EXTERMINATOR, Ignius Ellis's dream is to buy a candy-apple red Nova Supreme. In the process of trying to earn enough cash to make his dream come true he gets sucked into the rough world of Visitacion Valley, SF. When the tenants in his apartment complex reveal their various extracurricular activities this take an even more bizarre twist and Ellis soon becomes acquainted with the nightmarish Slave State dimension..."

THAT'S THE LAST TIME SHE GETS THE BIGGER WORM...

Once their flesh flakes away the angels collapse into
puddles of hissing goop and withered petals blow into
them hurried along by unseen winds. My spit looses its
sweet taste to the black flavor of ash. The glowing birds in
the bright orange sky burst into small sparkly novas. The
sky itself weeps and tears, streaking down like a ruined
painting as the dismal gray of life wheezes back before my
eyes. I don't blink; praying silently for one last desperate
sensation of the high. Lila feels it too. She writhes on the
mattress next to me; her moans of ecstasy warping into
groans that capture the hollowness of our souls. Tears
form in her eyes and I can almost feel the lump in her
throat. It's gone and she wants to cry. I'd rather chase

down more Worms than cry about it but everybody reacts to the Worms differently. I slip away to my own neon colored utopia where things with wings fan me and comfort me when the living neon worm dissolves under my skin. Lila told me once they wrap around her like a giant fuzzy neon hug. I imagine her high shedding off her like snake skin and flaking to the filthy floor next to the mattress. Her high sounds better than mine. More Fun. That's the last time she gets the bigger worm.

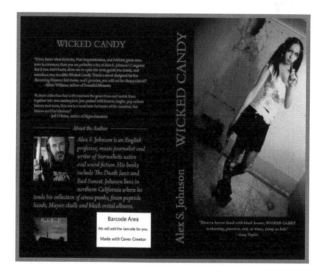

"IF YOU KNOW WHAT KINBAKU, POST-IMPRESSIONISM,
and brilliant green eyes have in common, then you are probably a fan of Alex S. Johnson! Congrats! But if you don't know, allow me to open the door, guide you inside,

and introduce you to a little Wicked Candy. This is a sweet designed for the discerning Bizarro fan's tastes, and I promise, you will not be disappointed!"

--Mimi Williams, author of Beautiful Monster

"A short collection that both traverses the genre lines and melds them together into one masterpiece. Jam packed with horror, laughs, pop culture history and more, this one is a must have for lovers of the macabre, the bizarre and the hilarious."

--Jeff O'Brien, author of Bigboobenstein

IN GARRETT COOK'S MURDERLAND serial killers are idolized by society. Their deeds are followed obsessively by

television pundits and the adoring public. A subculture
has grown up around this phenomena, called "Reap." Laws
are created to allow this activity to flourish, including
designated "safe zones' where killers can practice their
trade without fear of persecution. Fans of the top rated
serial killers celebrate each new kill on social media and
television. Programs glorify their deeds.

The culture of Murderland is violent and mirrors our own
violent society and its decadent obsessions; but
Murderland isn't about how violent the world has
become. It's about the pervasive nature of media and how
it corrupts. It corrupts absolutely.

At the heart of Murderland is Jeremy Jenkins. Jeremy
doesn't like what he sees and he's just enough insane to
believe he can do something about it, that he can change
the world. His methods are extreme- to outdo the serial
killers, he'll kill THEM, turn their own twisted reality back
on themselves. It's a hopeless task, impossible, Herculean;
but it's Jeremy's fate to see it through to the end.

The three sections of Murderland comprise a true
Homeric epic. In the first section we are shown the
terrible world Jeremy lives in, the world that if we look at
it honestly, is really our own world. We meet all the
principal characters, the serial killers, the pundits, the
pawns, and Jeremy's beloved Cass. In the second section
Jeremy goes on a bit of a spiritual quest and comes to

understand his true purpose. In the final section the flames are ignited and all hell breaks loose. Jeremy, like a great epic hero must journey to the underworld and be reborn in order to triumph.

BORN WHOLE FROM THE RECTUM of a dying patient, Morbid silently stalks the hospital's hallways, heinously dispatching the most helpless of patients and in the most painfully repulsive of manners. In the meantime, in order to pay for his family and home that includes his ghost step-father Sammy and his pet aborted fetus Chip, Westphal has to ingest mounds of dangerous narcotics to get through his night shifts. Barely hanging on to his Care Tech gig by his fingernails, the last thing Westphal needs is to be accused of Morbid's evil deeds. You, on the other hand, simply want to find some solace. Terminally ill from a virulent infection, and dependent on Life Support, all You beg for a peaceful and dignified demise. Shirk has other plans for You. The ancient drug-snuffling demon makes You relive all of your deadly and venial sins as he tortures You. Night after night. Until eternal Damnation begins for YOU MORBID WESTPHAL, yet again.... NOW WITH EVEN *MORE* EVIL FLAVOR!

IT LOOKS LIKE CAROLYN AND MARK

are in deep, deep shit...

Mark and Carolyn live in an alternate 1989 where Ronald Reagan is on his fourth presidential term. The USA has a rigid, long-standing caste system and abortions were never made legal. Being homeless is a crime that is punishable by imprisonment in an internment camp the inmates call Tent City. Most of Mark's ER patients are inmates at this camp and are victims of a new disease these illegals call the Transient Flu. This deadly and rapidly spreading disease mutates with each new host, collecting information, changing code. The disease evolves lightning quick, spreading like pond ripples and infecting everyone. No one is safe. Mark and Carolyn dig too deep and uncover the brutal truth: Transient Flu was purposely made and is one hundred percent fatal. Carolyn's employer, Hudson-Smythe Pharmaceuticals, discovers the chain of evidence. It traces the pharmacide back to Hudson-Smythe and the crime of the century. Cost is no object and deadly force is authorized. Yes. Carolyn and Mark are in deep, deep shit.

JORDAN KRALL

IMMANUEL THE CHRIST HAS SOME NERVE. Jonah has already lost everyone he loves to Pilate the vampire and his Harbor drug violence. Jonah now trudges through his days staying as high on Plata as possible. He just wants to be left alone while he waits for his turn to die. The Christ has other plans for him. She sends Her messenger, Pedro, to assign Jonah the very dangerous task of ordering the Herod to dismantle the Harbor's Plata trade. Jonah decides to run. But you can't run from God forever. As Jonah learns the hard way when the 'Edmund Fitzgerald' founders and goes down in rough seas, with the reluctant prophet on board. Job is Satan's Chosen One and he doesn't take kindly to orders from some upstart prophet.

Printed in Great Britain
by Amazon.co.uk, Ltd.,
Marston Gate.